Simply Irresistible

A Totally Sweet Love Story

By Jennifer L. Allen

Dedication

To the dreamers...
may all your dreams come true.

- 1 -
Tyler

"So I told her, 'Let me go get you a cape, then you can be *super angry*.'" I paused for added dramatic effect. "She slapped me."

"You're so charming," Hannah said, wiping the corner of her mouth with a napkin. "Oh! That's why you had that black eye!"

"No, *that* was from when I fell up the stairs on my way home from the bar. You're giving Nicole way too much credit."

"Tyler," Hannah sighed, and I waited for it. I waited for that inevitable moment in the lives of all single people when a coupled-up friend, relative, coworker, or complete stranger told you how unfortunate it was that you're still single, and how insane you must be that you couldn't make a relationship work. *You know what I mean.*

I tuned my sister out, having heard this spiel before, and took in the sights and sounds around me. Central Park was bustling at lunch time, as usual. Businessmen and women in their power suits speed walked down the dirt path on their way to some place important, parents held their children's hands as they made their way from one museum to another, and tourists with actual fanny packs snapped pictures left and right. Hannah and I were taking up prime real estate on a bench while we ate the turkey on wheat sandwiches. She painstakingly made our lunch (insert eyeroll) this morning after kissing her gazillionaire husband goodbye in their Park Avenue apartment. My older sister hit the jackpot, quite literally, back in the fifth grade when she met and fell in love with her now husband, Preston. Yes, they met and fell in love when they were ten. It was sickening...twenty years with just one person by age 30. *Blech. I'll pass.*

I looked across the expanse of green grass dotted with people and picnic blankets. There were some sunbathers scattered here and there, and I tried not to let my gaze linger too long on one particularly skimpy red and white polka dot bikini about thirty feet to my left. *Summer in New York City*, I mused to myself. Always something to look at...appreciate.

"Are you even listening to me?" Hannah asked, bringing me back to the present.

"No," I answered truthfully. She narrowed her eyes at me, and I swore I saw steam come out of her ears. *Here we go.*

"I just don't get it, Tyler. You're an attractive guy; you should have a steady girlfriend by now."

"It's not my fault all the women in Manhattan are crazy."

She rolled her eyes. "*All* the women in Manhattan are *not* crazy."

"Explain Marilyn to me then."

"I never said *she* wasn't crazy."

Marilyn was a waitress at a beer garden I used to frequent with some friends back in college. I dated her for about two weeks, and she was a wildcat. Things with Marilyn were hot. Then one Friday night, instead of going to the beer garden, my buddies decided to go to a pub in midtown, and she blew up my phone. I had eighty-seven missed calls, thirty-five voicemails, and two hundred and forty-six text messages. That all happened over the course of three hours. Needless to say, I broke up with her.

"Rose?" I asked, taking a bite of my sandwich.

"Rose wasn't crazy."

"She wasn't?" I looked up at the cloudless sky, trying to remember why I broke up with Rose.

"No, she dumped you when you told her you knew you liked her because you missed her even when you weren't horny."

I laughed. That was absolutely correct, I remembered it clearly. I *had* liked Rose for more than just sex.

"It's not funny, Tyler. Rose really liked you, and she was nice. Don't you see that you're the problem in these relationships."

I glared at my sister, the most recent bite of food turning to sand in my mouth. "You're supposed to be on my side."

"I am on your side. But I feel like you're self-sabotaging."

"Why do I even have to be in a relationship?" I asked, giving up on the rest of my sandwich and tossing the remains back into the brown paper bag she'd packed everything in. The turn our conversation had taken made me lose my appetite.

"Because, you need to have a person, Tyler."

"You're my person," I said. And I realized how pathetic those words were the moment they left my lips.

Hannah gave me a sad smile. It was the same sad smile I'd seen on her face every time I reminded her that she was the only family I had left in the world since our parents' deaths ten years ago. "I'll always be here for you. You know that. But you need someone who is more than me. You need real intimacy in your life."

"And on that note," I said, looking at my watch, "I have to get back to work." I did have to return to work before my asshole boss had a conniption fit, but I mostly needed to leave that conversation.

Hannah sighed again, this time a sigh of defeat, and started cleaning up. I helped, then dropped the bag of trash into a nearby garbage can, sneaking one last peek at the polka dot bikini before returning to my sister. I gave her a kiss on the cheek.

"Thanks for lunch."

"Of course," she said, pulling me in for one of her patented big sister hugs. Growing up, they always made me feel better. This one had that same effect today. "I love you, little brother."

"Love you, too, Han." I gave her a quick wave before I took off through the park, knowing if I was even half a second late, I'd be filleted. I ran straight through Columbus Circle towards West 57th where the headquarters for the magazine were located. I made it into the elevator with four minutes to spare, having barely broken a sweat. Those morning runs were really paying off.

I was so impressed with myself that I didn't even realize I had company in the elevator until I caught a flash of pink out of the corner of my eye. I looked over and met the eyes of my elevator companion.

It was *her*.

I'd seen this woman before. She worked in the

building—obviously—I thought for *Leading Lady*, the sister magazine of *You're the Man*. I'd seen her get off on that floor before; it was right below mine. She was cute, with big greenish-brown eyes and thick, jet black hair that framed her round face and fell just past her shoulders. Her dark hair and olive skin tone were a sharp contrast to her pale pink skirt suit that perfectly matched her plump lips. She was also tall, which was refreshing for a guy like me who was six-foot-five. In her heels, she was only an inch or so shorter than me.

I gave her a nod of acknowledgement, not wanting to startle her by speaking. She seemed shy, almost painfully so, sticking hard to the opposite corner of the large elevator. I wished she'd make eye contact. I would have liked to see her eyes again. I'd never seen a shade of green like that before. I wanted to study her eyes.

The bell on the elevator dinged and my mystery woman stepped out of the car without so much as a parting glance. I would have been offended if I wasn't certain that it was just the shyness. The doors closed and the elevator rose one more level to my floor. I closed my eyes, straightened my tie and suit jacket, and then exited when the doors opened.

Mystery woman already forgotten.

It was back to hell.

- 2 -
Melanie

I must have turned twelve different shades of red on that elevator. I *felt* his stare like a caress, and it only made my skin heat more. *Gah!* Why did I have to be so socially awkward?

I bumped into the mail cart, muttering an apology as I hurried through the city of cubicles, back towards my suite. Brianna Heatherly, the Editor in Chief of *Leading Lady* magazine, was my boss. She was the only person on this floor with their own suite. She was also a wonderful woman and an even better editor, but she was firm, and if I was late returning from lunch, she'd treat me the same way she treated every other staffer here...with an iron fist.

I will not be late.

I slipped in the door, dropped my bottom in my chair, swung my legs under the desk, and shook the mouse, waking up my computer. I plugged in my username and password and the computer screen changed to show my busy desktop screen just as Brianna pushed open the French doors to her office.

"Melanie," she said as she stepped through the doorway in a pair of pressed black slacks and a red flowy top that I was sure was handpicked for her by some designer. Her blond hair was cut in a severe bob, barely moving as her icy blue eyes locked on mine. "I need you to cancel my afternoon. Please reschedule everything you can for some point later this week." She turned around before I could acknowledge her request/demand, then stopped. "Actually, see if you can get Bradley back on the schedule as soon as possible." Bradley was a representative from Jason Red, the new "it" designer who had a huge spread in an upcoming issue.

"Anything else, Brianna?"

She peeked over her shoulder, her eyes moving over me. "You look cute today," she said with a barely perceptible smile, then disappeared behind closed doors again.

I smiled and got to work sending off emails and texts to the assistants of the people on Brianna's schedule for this afternoon. To make my job easier, when I'd started working for Brianna four years ago, I reached out to the assistants of her business associates. In many organizations, it was the assistants who did most of the work. Sure, the execs made the deals and decisions, but the assistants were the ones who made the appointments to discuss the deals. The assistants greased the wheels. So one week, while Brianna was in Milan for a fashion show, I called every single assistant and introduced myself. A handful of them hung up on me, angry with me for wasting their time, but the majority of them appreciated the effort. Being Brianna's assistant held some clout, after all. I never did forget the ones who hung up on me, and every now and then I have some fun with that. Brianna was widely known around the fashion industry and everyone wanted to be on her good side, and therefore…my good side. Over the years, I developed acquaintanceships with some of the assistants and we learned each other's preferred forms of communications. Like I knew for a fact that Billie, assistant to this fabulous makeup artist, would rather me send her a text than call unless it was a dire emergency. Brianna needing to reschedule her three o'clock was *not* an emergency. And Jonathan, personal assistant to supermodel Leigha Morelli, preferred email because he has some anal-retentive filing system. By the time I was finished shooting off messages to the others, Jonathan had already replied that the same time tomorrow, which Brianna was also available for, worked for Leigha. I adjusted Brianna's digital schedule to reflect the change. *Perfect.*

As I waited for the rest of the replies to roll in, my mind drifted back to the guy in the elevator. Oh boy, was he delicious. I'd seen him in the elevator enough to know he must work somewhere in the building. Whenever I saw him, I didn't see which floor he got off at, so I guessed he worked on one of the upper levels. But where? I tapped a few keys on my computer and pulled up the building's directory. Parks Publishing, Inc., the parent company of *Leading Lady* magazine, had several subsidiaries throughout the building, including *You're the Man, Move Your Body,* and *Baby Stuff.* It was probably the most awfully named collection of magazines, but the owner, Preston Parks, was a billionaire, so I didn't think he cared what I thought of the names of his magazines because they obviously worked. *You're the Man* was one floor up, beyond that was a marketing firm, an ad agency, and a law firm. He was dressed for any one of those in his light gray suit, which he filled out nicely, too. He was taller than me, which was a plus, with lean muscles—his suit jacket snugly fit around his chest, shoulders and biceps, the fabric stretched ever so much. Mmm. His face was nice to look at, too. His short, light brown hair was done in that purposefully messy way guys always got away with. His blue eyes sparkled as he looked at me, his full lips transforming into a smirk just before he'd nodded at me. I blushed just remembering it. *Why do I have to be so awkward?* It had been a decent opportunity to chat up a new guy—a new *gorgeous* guy—and I screwed it up.

My dating life had suffered since moving to Manhattan after college. It was never all that active to begin with but being a tiny speck in the ocean of a city that was New York did absolutely nothing to help me come out of my shell. If I was shy before, I didn't know what I was considered now. At work, I was cool and confident. When I was sitting behind my desk, I knew what was expected of me. When I went out into the world...anything could happen. It was both wonderful and terrifying all at once. I just kept my head low and did what I had to do. So yes, it made it very difficult to meet new people.

Speaking of people...my phone pinged with a new text message, and this time it was from my best friend, Meredith.

Meredith: What's happening, City Girl?
Melanie: Just another day. How about you?
Meredith: Same old.
Melanie: Well, this is riveting but…

Meredith: I might have gotten engaged this weekend.

Was she kidding me right now??

Melanie: And you're texting me?!?!
Meredith: Well, I know that you're at work!
Melanie: And how about the moment after you said yes??

Seriously, didn't she understand the first rule of girls' club? Well...maybe it wasn't the first rule. Okay, maybe there wasn't a rule at all, but still. I couldn't believe she waited a full day to tell me, and then she told me via text message.

Meredith: We were sort of up to other things then.
Melanie: You're gross.
Meredith: It's only gross because you've been single forever.

Ouch.

Meredith: I'm sorry, I didn't mean that.
Melanie: Yes, you did.
Meredith: Any prospects?

I thought about telling Meredith about the guy in the elevator. Then I remembered that I couldn't even make eye contact with him, and there was nothing really to tell. I heard Brianna stirring in her office.

Melanie: No. Look, I've got to get back to work, but expect a Facetime call when I get home from work!
Meredith: Roger dodger.

I tucked my phone back into my desk drawer right as Brianna stuck her head out of her office. "Any word from Bradley?"

"He'll be here tomorrow morning at eleven." I'd just received an email back from his assistant confirming the change.

"Perfect. You are an angel, Melanie."

She disappeared again, and I reclined in my chair, looking up at the fluorescent lights above my desk. This wasn't my dream job, but it was a foot in the door of the fashion world, and I was damn good at it.

At that moment...that was enough for me.

- 3 -
Tyler

"I really don't think it's that difficult of a concept to understand, Scott. When she calls, tell her I'm in a meeting."

Reason four-hundred-thirty-eight why I hated my boss…he called me by my last name. I wasn't sure if it was because he called everyone by their last name — because he did that, too — or if it was because he was just a dick.

Reason seventeen why I hated my boss — I learned this one early on — he was a cheating pig and didn't deserve his sweet wife, who he was asking me to lie to for the thousandth time while he went out with some girl half his age. Roger Hoffstadt was in his mid-forties, balding, with a beer belly and a peaked in high school vibe. *You're the Man* didn't use female models very often, and when they did, Roger had nothing to do with it, so why this girl and the others before her wasted their time with him, I'd never understand. He wouldn't and couldn't get them in the industry the way they wanted.

He left with the too thin girl hanging on his arm and as soon as the elevator doors slid closed behind them, I popped earbuds in my ear, choosing a nineties pop playlist on Amazon Music. Spice Girl's "Wannabe" started playing, and I was immediately in my happy place. There was nothing the nineties couldn't cure, in my opinion.

I worked all morning, making notes on article submissions and reviewing ad copy; things Roger was supposed to do yet never did. He reviewed what I put on his desk and approved my changes, rarely ever making additional edits or giving me proper credit. I didn't care though, not really. This job was just a stepping stone to a career as a journalist. I wanted to be the one writing the articles and making the submissions. I wanted to see my work with red ink splattered all over it…well, maybe not *all* over it.

I only thought about elevator girl once. It had been two days since I'd seen her last and I wondered when I'd see her again. I decided I'd ask her to lunch the next time I saw her.

Speaking of lunch…I paused my music app and pulled out my earbuds, deciding it was a good time to eat. I logged off my computer and stood, pocketing my cell phone. Since Roger was out of the office, I didn't have to report my departure to anyone, so I took off across the floor towards the elevator, weaving through the dozen or so cubicles filled with writers and ad staff.

Someday, I promised myself, *you will be part of the pit.*

Once in the elevator, I punched the lobby button and the doors closed. I watched the numbers change on the small screen above the doors as the elevator descended, then paused at the floor below.

Could it be? I hoped it was her…

The doors opened, and a couple models walked on barely sparing me a glance. I took offense to it in the beginning…the whole being blown off thing. I'd always thought I was a good-looking guy, and when these women wouldn't even look my way, it was a major blow to my ego. Then I realized that most of the models were so self-absorbed (or hungry) that they didn't pay attention to anyone around them, not even male models, so it wasn't just me. Ego restored.

Just as the doors were about to meet in the middle, a slim hand slipped between them, causing them to reopen. I was met with those wide greenish-brown eyes, and I couldn't help but smile. She smiled back. What was odd was that both models smiled and said hello to her when she stepped inside.

Who was she?

My mystery woman looked like a pin-up girl. She was wearing a black dress with a high neckline. It fit tightly around her chest and flared out from her waist, stopping just above her knees. She had a long, hot pink scarf tied around her trim waist. She sidled up beside me, giving me another shy smile, another peek at those beautiful eyes. I wanted to ask her to lunch right now, but I didn't want to do it with an audience. What if she spooked? Or turned me down in front of people? So, I waited. I wanted nine whole floors, three of which we stopped at. As soon as we reached the lobby and the car unloaded, I reached for her arm.

"Excuse me?" I said softly, and she turned to look at me, a question in her eyes. "I'm Tyler," I said, feeling like an idiot, but knowing I had to at least tell her my name before I asked her out.

"Melanie," she said, and I smiled again. Her voice was soft and angelic. Well, maybe a little huskier than an angel, but still sexy.

"It's nice to officially meet you, Melanie." Her cheeks pinked when she realized I'd noticed her before that moment. "I'm heading to lunch, and I was wondering if you'd like to join me."

She looked towards the door briefly, as if seeking out an escape route, and my heart sunk. Then she looked back to me, her cheeks redder than before, and she smiled a beautiful smile.

"I'd like that."

I exhaled the breath I'd been holding and returned her smile. "Great. There's a little Thai place up the road that's pretty quick."

"Thai Two?" she asked.

"You know it?" I asked, turning towards the door.

She fell into step beside me. "Know it? I think I've probably single-handedly kept their delivery guy in business over the last couple years."

"Ah, I've never ordered delivery from them." She looked at me, surprised. "I prefer to leave for lunch." I almost said *escape,* but I held back since I wasn't sure what her role was yet with *Leading Lady.* No matter how much of an asshole I thought he was, I wasn't about to bad mouth my boss to one of his colleagues. I had a great reputation at *You're the Man* and I wasn't about to ruin that.

She nodded, and we exited the building onto the crowded city street. The heat hit me as soon as I'd stepped outside, that and the smell of pretzels and hot dogs from the nearby street vendors. It made my stomach growl, and I was thankful we were headed to lunch.

"What do you do at *Leading Lady?*" I asked, breaking the silence as we waited on the corner for the signal to walk.

"I'm Brianna Heatherly's executive assistant." I stared at her, speechless for a moment. This girl was the equivalent to *me* at her magazine, executive assistant to the editor-in-chief. The reaction from the models made sense now. Melanie was a gatekeeper.

"Wow, that's pretty cool."

She shrugged off my comment as we crossed the street. "What do you do?" she asked.

"I'm actually the executive assistant to the editor-in-chief of *You're the Man*."

Her eyebrows went up. "You work for Roger Hoffstadt?"

"I do," I said, wanting to deny it.

"I'm so sorry," she said, then she slapped her hand over her mouth, and her eyes went wide, like she couldn't believe she'd said the words aloud.

I couldn't help but laugh. "I take it Roger's reputation is well known?"

She made a face. "There's a lot of talk around the water cooler about him." I shook my head, surprised he still had a job given his notoriety. "I'm sorry," she apologized again.

"No need to apologize," I told her, stepping ahead to pull open the restaurant door.

"But if you like him…"

I laughed at that. "I don't like him, Spice. Not even a little bit." She frowned, and I could tell she wanted to say more but we were interrupted by the hostess.

We were escorted to a small table in the back, and I held out Melanie's chair for her. Her long hair moved over her shoulder, and I caught scent of strawberries and peaches. It smelled delicious — *she* smelled delicious.

- 4 -
Melanie

"Why do you work for Roger if you don't like him?" I asked once we'd placed our orders.

"You don't waste any time, do you, Spice?" I looked down, embarrassed by my boldness. I felt his finger under my chin, lifting it. "I'm just messing with you," he said, smiling. "I want to be a writer--a journalist--this job just got me in the door. Something to look good on my resume."

"So you're like the male version of Andy Sachs."

"Andy who?"

"Andy Sachs...*The Devil Wears Prada*?" How could he work in the industry and not know who she was?

"I guess so," he said, shrugging.

I raised my eyebrow. "You've never seen it?"

He shook his head. "No. I prefer nineties movies."

"Nineties movies?" Who actually liked nineties movies? "Were there any good nineties movies?" I asked with a laugh.

"Were there any good nineties movies?" he scoffed. "*Pulp Fiction, Jurassic Park, Forrest Gump, Clueless, Home Alone, Titanic, The Matrix*...need I go on?"

I shrugged. "Those are some good films, but the eighties totally beat the nineties for entertainment."

"Excuse me?" he shrieked. The waitress, who had been placing our plates on the table at that very moment, jumped back. "Sorry," he told her. "Not you."

I thanked the server, then looked at Tyler. "The eighties had better movies."

"I beg to differ," he interrupted. He looked…green…but I didn't let that deter me.

"*Back to the Future, The Goonies, E.T., The Breakfast Club, Ferris Bueller's Day Off, Ghostbusters*, and, my favorite, *Stand by Me*. Those are only a handful of the best movies ever. Don't even get me started on the music."

"And what's wrong with nineties music? N*Sync and the Backstreet Boys started in the nineties. Chicks love that shit." I narrowed my eyes at him, and he apologized.

"I don't really like boy bands," I told him, and he winced liked I'd slapped him.

Was this really happening? Did someone put me up to this? Meredith? I started to look around for someone I knew. I was being punked. It was the only explanation. This was the weirdest date I'd ever been on, if I could even call it that. The super-hot guy from the elevator finally spoke to me, asked me to lunch and I didn't stumble over my words, then he turned out to be a complete weirdo.

Several awkward moments passed and neither of us said a word, or made eye contact. When I wasn't scanning the restaurant for a camera crew, I studied my nails. He was staring down at the table. He looked sick…maybe a little constipated. Was he breathing?

"Are you okay?" I asked him. He still looked green. More so than before.

He shook his head. "I was just expecting this to go differently, I guess."

"Yeah, me too." I put my napkin on the table, having lost my appetite. "You're pretty passionate about the nineties."

"You're pretty passionate about the eighties," he said, leaning back in his seat.

We stared at each other across the table, the ridiculousness of the situation settling between us. I wasn't sure who laughed first, but pretty soon we were both in hysterics.

"I'm pretty sure my love for nineties pop culture is on my sister's top ten list for why my relationships fail," Tyler confessed once we got ourselves under control.

"That bad, huh?" I asked.

He raised an eyebrow at me. "I believe you're the one who said 'don't even get me started on the music.'"

"Touché."

He looked at his watch, causing me to do the same. I noted that my lunch hour was almost over.

"Can we maybe try this again sometime?" His question surprised me. Our lunch had been a disaster, and yet he wanted to do it again? He must have read my expression because he smiled and shook his head, looking down at his half-eaten plate. "Look at that…we survived our first argument. Next time we get together, we'll know not to talk about movies or music."

I laughed softly. Did I want to see him again? Yes, I did. Despite his terrible taste in music — boy bands? really? — he seemed like a nice guy. He was attractive and we had some things in common, like our jobs and our desire to do something more than what we were currently doing.

"I'd like to see you again," I told him, and I was glad I did because his eyes lit up a bright blue. He was so handsome.

"Can I get your number? We could try to run into each other in the elevator again, but I'd kind of like to see you when we don't have a time limit." He held out his cell phone. I smiled and took the phone, tapping in my number. He laughed when he looked at what I'd entered. "Eighties Girl?"

I shrugged. "Seemed appropriate. Wanted to make sure you remembered."

"I don't think I'd ever forget," he said. And something told me he was talking about more than just our little decade feud.

***

"What's happening, chica?"

"Hey, Mer. Nothing much." I turned my cell phone to speaker mode and set it beside me on my bed. I was sketching out some new designs and wanted to keep my hands free.

"How's work?"

"The same."

"You're sketching, aren't you?"

"Yep."

"I knew it. You always give me short answers when you're sketching."

"I'm sorry, Mer. I just got this great idea for a new collection the other day, and I haven't been able to stop."

"That's great, Mel. Have you showed your stuff to Brianna yet?"

"No," I said, knowing she'd give me grief for it. Meredith had been bugging me to show Brianna my ideas for ages. She had the utmost confidence in my talent and was certain Brianna would hook me up with my own spread in the very next issue of *Leading Lady*. Meredith had *no idea* how it worked in the fashion industry. I'd been working in it for two years and *I* was still unsure.

"Come on, Mel. What are you waiting for?"

I couldn't answer that because I really didn't know what I was waiting for. I didn't fully understand the system, but I knew I had to start somewhere. And Brianna *was* a great place to start. "I wear some of my designs to work, Mer. If Brianna was interested, she'd say something." That wasn't entirely true. Brianna would have to pay attention to what I was wearing enough to notice it. She may have said I looked cute the other day, but I wasn't wearing one of my designs that day, so it was irrelevant.

Meredith sighed. "What else is new?"

"I sort of went on a date."

"What?!" she shrieked, and I grimaced at the phone. "Why was this not the first thing you said to me?"

"It didn't come up?"

"I asked you 'what's happening?' That's a general question that encompasses all recent activities. I'm pretty sure a date would classify as something *happening*. Tell me everything!"

I set down my pencil and rolled onto my back on my twin-sized bed—it was all that would fit in my tiny studio apartment. I was all about saving money so I'd have a cushion for when I finally launched my own fashion label. It would happen, one day. Some day. Somehow.

"It was awkward," I admitted.

"Of course, it was," she groaned. "What did you do?"

"I didn't do anything." And I didn't. Not really. He started it…

"You went all crazy eighties on him, didn't you?"

"He went all crazy nineties on me first!"

"What? That's a thing?"

"That's what I said."

"Am I getting this right? You had a date with a guy who is hooked on the nineties the way you're hooked on the eighties?"

"I'm not hook-"

"Answer the question, Melanie."

"Yes," I said, not a hint of defiance in my voice. Not at all.

"Aw, you found another decade geek. How cute! Maybe he's your soulmate!"

I rolled my eyes. "On that note. It's late, I'm going to bed."

"It's not late! It's not even ten."

"Good night, Meredith."

"You're not getting off that easily, Mel! I'll see you soon! We need to go dress scouting!"

"Yeah, okay. Bye, Mer!" I tapped the end button and rolled to my side, resting my head on my hands.

Was Meredith right? Had I found my soul-geek?

- 5 -
Tyler

I watched *The Devil Wears Prada*. My only takeaway from the movie was that I wished Roger was more like Meryl Streep's character. At least she eventually acknowledged that her assistant was competent. I could only be so lucky, I supposed. I was blessed with good looks, so I obviously wasn't going to have a great boss, too.

It had been four days since my date with Melanie, and I wanted to see her again. I decided that telling her I watched the movie was the perfect opening and sent her a text when Roger left the office with his girl of the day.

Tyler: I watched The Devil Wears Prada. I wish Miranda Priestly was my boss.

Eighties Girl: LOL That's very telling. I'm adding your name in my phone as "Andy Sachs."

Tyler: I'm changing your name from "Eighties Girl" to "Mean Girl."

Eighties Girl: Oh wow, isn't that a 2000s pop culture reference?

Tyler: Huh?

Eighties Girl: Nevermind. How about I just call you Tyler and you call me Melanie.

Tyler: I like that idea.

I changed her name in my phone. *Melanie.*

What were the chances her name would be
Melanie? My favorite Spice Girl was named
Melanie.

> Melanie: I like it, too.
> Tyler: Are you free this week for our second date?
> Melanie: What did you have in mind?
> Tyler: Not dinner and a movie…
> Melanie: LOL Good call.

A thought suddenly came to me, and I wasn't
sure how I hadn't thought of it before. We didn't
have the obligatory sports conversation. All
serious New Yorkers picked sides. It could make
or break a relationship…none of that house
divided crap.

> Tyler: Wait…I can't believe I didn't ask you this the
> other day…Yankees or Mets?
> Melanie: Wow. I also can't believe we didn't get this
> out of the way. Mets. You?
> Tyler: Mets. Giants or Jets?
> Melanie: Eh. Neither. I prefer hockey. And before
> you ask, the Rangers. The only New York hockey team.
> Tyler: Phew. This could have been over before it even
> started. I am a little disappointed you don't like football,
> but I can live with that since you've got good taste in
> hockey.
> Melanie: Yes, we definitely dodged a bullet. The
> Rangers were ingrained in me at a young age.
> Tyler: Me too.
> Melanie: Your parents fans?
> Tyler: They were.
> Melanie: Were?
> Tyler: They passed away.

Melanie: I'm so sorry, Tyler.
Tyler: Thanks.

Way to go, Ty. Mood killer.

Tyler: About that date…
Melanie: Yes?
Tyler: When should I pick you up?
Melanie: How about Thursday at 7:00?
Tyler: That works for me. I'm going to be honest.
Sometimes I get stuck working late for my asshole boss.
I'll text you if that happens, but I wanted to let you
know in advance in case it happens.
Melanie: I appreciate that.
Melanie: We can always meet in the lobby after
work?
Tyler: No. I want to do this right. Let me pick you
up?
Melanie: Of course.
Tyler: Perfect. I need to get back to work, but text me
your address and if I don't see you in the elevator before
then, I'll see you Thursday.
Melanie: Looking forward to it.

I plugged in my earbuds and went to my music
app. My fingertip hovered over the search field,
but I couldn't do it. I couldn't step outside my
perfectly crafted music box. The eighties were *not*
better than the nineties, so really there was no
point at all. In fact, I was going to make Melanie a
mix tape. What a *nineties* thing for me to do. I'd
give it to her on our date and she'd love it. I'd
make her a nineties girl yet.

***

"That was so much fun," Melanie gushed as we walked out onto the sidewalk.

"I'm glad you liked it," I said, taking her hand and leading her in the direction of the restaurant where we'd have a late dinner. She blushed again; it was a good look on her. She was dressed plainly, as I'd suggested when I texted her earlier that day, in dark jeans and a teal short-sleeve shirt. She dressed the outfit up with some jewelry and fancy, gold sandals. She looked amazing, but she'd look good in a potato sack. "I figured it was better than a movie," I winked at her, and she smiled.

"I've never done an escape room before. I thought I'd feel claustrophobic or something, but I didn't. Not at all."

"I did one once with my sister."

"Are you two close?" she asked.

"Very. She's older than me by a few years. She…uh…she took me in when my parents passed away."

Melanie squeezed my hand. "I'm so sorry you lost them, Tyler."

"Thanks," I squeezed her hand back and moved to the right side of the sidewalk as we approached the restaurant. "I hope you like Greek." This place had the best gyros.

Melanie laughed. "I *am* Greek, of course, I like Greek food."

Oh shit. Wasn't there some unspoken rule that you never ever took someone to the ethnic restaurant that was their ethnicity? Like bringing an Italian to an Italian restaurant? Or a Greek to a cheap gyro place?

Melanie laughed, the sound like tinkling bells.

"I see that look on your face. Stop panicking. I'm not a Greek food snob, I promise."

"Are you sure? Because we can go somewhere else."

"I'm positive," she said and tugged me through the open door.

It wasn't a fancy place. We placed our orders at the counter and found a table where we waited for our number to be called. Melanie told me about growing up with her huge Greek family on Long Island, and I told her what it was like living with my sister and her husband in Manhattan. She was as fascinated as everyone else when I told her how long Hannah and her husband had been together.

"Since fifth grade? Like twenty years already? Wow! That's amazing."

"She always tells people 'When you know, you know.'"

"I guess so. That's amazing."

"That's one person for your entire life." I said and immediately regretted the words. Maybe Hannah was right, maybe I did self-sabotage. But maybe I didn't realize I did it.

Melanie just rolled with it. "But that's what fits for her and her husband. I think if I'd found *the* guy in the first guy I'd ever dated, then I'd probably be content only ever being with him. I'd feel fulfilled, you know? If I had everything I needed in a partner, I wouldn't want anything else. There'd be no lusting for another man because I'd have it all. And, well, if I did lust for someone else, then it wasn't meant to be."

Was that what my problem was? Was I still lusting after something? I looked at the beautiful woman sitting across the table from me in this dive restaurant, smiling at me like I'd taken her to some five-star place. I didn't feel like I wanted anything else in that moment. I felt…good…complete.

"Oh," I said remembering about the tape. I pulled a cassette tape out of my back pocket and slid it over the table to her. "I made you a mix tape."

She looked at the plastic cartridge on the table like she'd never seen one before in her life. But I knew she had, we established that we graduated high school one year apart, so we were close in age. If I knew what it was, so did she.

"Wow," she said, and I wasn't sure if it was a good wow or a bad wow. "It's so very nineties of you to make me a mix tape."

I let out a breath at that. She was teasing me. That was good. "That's exactly what I thought when I decided to make it."

She laughed.
She was good.
We were good.
Everything was good.

- 6 -
Melanie

One thing I could say about Tyler's taste in music was that he sure was eclectic, especially considering it was all nineties. It flipped from "No Scrubs" by TLC to "Lovefool" by The Cardigans and several oddities in between. It wasn't *terrible*, just weird. I hadn't heard Ini Kamoze in years; talk about a blast from the past!

I'd had a great time on our date the other night. I loved how Tyler kept the evening low key with the escape room and a simple dinner, it was like he knew I'd be anxious with something fancier. I honestly wasn't quite sure how I was able to keep it together. On a scale of one to ten, my baseline nerves were usually a five in social situations, but with him I was just comfortable. I couldn't explain it.

I stepped off the train in Port Jefferson and peered through the crowd, looking for Meredith. We were meeting today to look at wedding dresses. She wasn't in a rush to get married, didn't even have a date picked out yet, but she told me she'd always dreamed about her wedding dress and couldn't wait another second to go try some on. As long as she didn't make me try on anything hideous, I didn't mind one bit. I spotted Meredith's curly red hair just as she saw me and waved. I ran up to her and gave her a big hug. It had been a few months since I'd last seen her, and I'd missed my friend.

"You look amazing," she said, stepping back and looking me up and down. "Is this one of yours?" she asked, gesturing to my dress. It was a yellow sundress with cap sleeves and some white lacing around the waist and the hemline.

"Yeah. It's not part of any of the collections I've been working on recently, just something I put together."

"Just something I put together," she mimicked. "Well, it's fabulous. You look happy, too."

"Thanks; so do you. Being engaged seems to agree with you." Meredith grinned, then fanned herself with her left hand, showing off the huge rock on her ring finger. "Let me see that!" I said, grabbing her hand. Wow, the diamond had to be two carats. Keith, her fiancé, had spared no expense.

"He did good, right?"

"He did good," I confirmed. "It's beautiful."

"Thank you. What is that?"

"Huh?" I looked around for what she was talking about.

"That," she pointed, "hanging out of your bag."

"Oh, it's my Walkman," I said, tucking it deeper into my bag so it didn't fall out.

"Your *Walkman*? You still have one of those? Of course, you do. I can't believe you still listen to cassette tapes, Mel." She turned and began walking to the parking lot. I followed behind her as she continued her monologue. "You know they make those old albums of yours on CD. You can even buy them digitally, then you wouldn't have to worry about storing the tapes. You don't have a lot of space in your tiny apartment; I'm surprised you would waste space like that."

I rolled my eyes. "I'll have you know I don't have some massive collection of cassette tapes lurking beneath my bed as you seem to think." I did still have a small handful of cassette tapes but only of the things I hadn't been able to find on iTunes. They were tucked neatly underneath my bed with my Walkman for easy access when I needed a fix. "I have my Walkman today because Tyler made me a mix tape."

Meredith stopped in her tracks and spun to face me. "Are you for real right now?"

"What?"

"He made you a mix tape?"

"So what?" I said, starting to feel defensive. "I happened to think it was a very sweet gesture."

"That might be the most adorable thing I've ever heard. I mean, it wouldn't be if you two weren't…well…nerdy like that, but since you are, it's so cute!"

"I don't know if I should thank you or be offended."

Meredith waved off my comment and continued walking. "It was a compliment, Mel. You guys sound like a great match. So what was on the mix tape?"

"Nineties music. Some of his favorites, I guess."

"Like what?"

"Spice Girls and the Backstreet Boys." Those who were the last two bands I'd heard before getting off the train.

She stopped again. "Spice Girls and Backstreet Boys?"

"There's some Metallica and Nirvana on it,

too." She started walking again. "I want to make him an eighties mix, but I don't have a stereo to do it on."

"Or you can do what all the cool kids are doing these days and make a playlist on Spotify."

"Or I can do that."

"So you had a nice date?" she asked once we were settled in the car.

"Yeah. We had a really nice time, and it was casual, which was great. I was comfortable. I didn't feel like I had to put on a show, you know?"

"I don't miss that about dating at all. Always feeling like you're up for a job interview."

"Exactly! It felt so familiar, like we already knew each other." A thought occurred to me and I deflated. "You don't think we've friend-zoned each other, do you?"

Meredith looked at me quickly, then back at the road. "Why would you think that?"

"I don't know…maybe we're *too* comfortable with each other. Shouldn't there be jitters or something?"

"You two aren't getting married; you're just dating. You were probably a little nervous before your date, right?" I nodded; I had been nervous. "Well, there are your jitters. You can't expect them to last throughout the entire date. It's great that you two were comfortable with each other. That's a good sign."

"I guess so."

"When are you seeing him again?"

"Wednesday, he invited me over. He's going to cook."

Meredith wriggled her eyebrows. "Sounds nice."

I blushed. "It's not what you're thinking. We're not *there* yet."

"Uh huh."

We arrived at the bridal shop, and I was glad to not be the center of attention anymore. The bridal consultants fawned all over Meredith, and she ate it up. They sat us on a sofa with champagne flutes while they scurried around the store grabbing a variety of white princess gowns. Meredith yayed and nayed the designs and eventually disappeared into a dressing room with one of the consultants. While I waited, I pulled my sketch pad out of my bag and started playing around. I'd never tried designing a wedding dress before, but I was inspired by all the tulle I'd seen in the last half hour. I paused in my sketching to critique each dress Meredith tried on. None of them were doing the trick, and she finally left the dressing room back in her own clothes, disappointed at not finding exactly what she wanted.

"I'm ready for some lunch. Whatcha got there?" she asked, looking at the sketch pad. Meredith was one of the only people I ever let see my designs, so I handed the pad over. "Oh my God, Mel. This is amazing."

I shrugged. "It's just a little something I was playing with."

"Just a little something? Mel. This is everything I want in a dress."

"Well, yeah. I paid attention to what you liked and didn't like when they were showing you the gowns." Meredith just stared at me, open-mouthed.

"Miss Lane," the consultant called from the front counter, getting Meredith's attention.

Meredith walked over to the consultant, and I packed up my things.

"I want you to make my dress," Meredith said once we were seated in her car.

"What? No." One bad day of dress shopping and she had completely lost her mind.

"Yes. Melanie. You are making my dress. That," she said, gesturing to my bag and the sketchpad she knew was inside, "was my dress."

"I can't make your wedding dress, Mer."

"Why not?"

I puffed out a breath. *Why not?* I *could* make Meredith's dress. I had the skills. I went to school for it. I just needed to get the right fabric, the measurements…*I was going to make Meredith's wedding dress.*

"Okay, I'll do it."

"You will?" I nodded, and Meredith *whooped.* "Thank you so much!" She hugged me, and we laughed. "I just know whatever you come up with is going to be perfect."

No pressure.

- 7 -
Tyler

"I like your tiny apartment," Melanie said. The twinkling lights on the rooftop patio of my building made her eyes sparkle.

"Thanks," I said, not sure if she was being serious or not. It was incredibly small. Like four hundred square feet.

"It's bigger than mine," she added, and I raised my eyebrows in surprise. "By like half." She took another sip from her bottle. I'd bought wine just in case, but she opted for an ice-cold beer instead.

"That's hard to believe," I said. "I thought my apartment was the smallest in New York."

She laughed. "It's close, but I've got you beat. My entire building was remodeled a couple years ago, and all the units were broken down into tiny apartments. I have enough room for a twin-sized bed, a recliner, and a desk. I have a small refrigerator and microwave, too, and a private bathroom. Each floor has shared spaces, and there are full kitchens there. I don't use that too much, it's a little…"

"Weird?" I finished for her.

She smiled. "Yeah. Definitely weird. I usually order take-out or pick up microwave dinners. Occasionally I'll crave something homemade and use the kitchen, but I've got a few of my own pots, pans, and utensils. There's only so far I'll go with communal stuff and using pots and pans after a stranger is way beyond my comfort level."

"You're not friendly with your neighbors?" I asked as I flipped our steaks on the grill.

"I am," she quickly answered. "It's just that a couple of them don't speak English, so aside from the occasional smile and wave in the hallway, we don't really talk. And the other two units are short-term leases, I think, because people keep rotating through them."

"There are a couple units on my floor like that, too. I think they might actually be used as Airbnbs."

"Ah, maybe that's what the ones in my building are, too."

I pulled the steaks off the grill and set them on a plate to rest. Then I shut down the grill and started cleaning up. Melanie started to help me. "No, you're my guest. Please, have a seat at the table. I'll be right there."

She smiled shyly and took her beer over to the table. The roof of my building had a pretty nice set up. There was a large grill, an outdoor stove, an outdoor dining set, and a firepit surrounded by comfortable outdoor chairs. I reserved the table for tonight, but anyone could come up and use the other amenities. Regardless, it was a quiet outdoor space in Manhattan, high above the busy streets. We could enjoy the warm summer evening semi-privately.

"Those smell and look delicious," she said as I plated the steaks and put them on the table.

"Thank you." I hadn't ever cooked for a date before, so this was a first. In addition to the steaks, I grilled some zucchini and yellow squash;

something else I'd never done before. I hoped I was doing a good job with this whole thing. I didn't just want to impress Melanie, I wanted…I didn't know what I wanted exactly. I just wanted *more* with her. I watched her cut into her steak and lift the fork to her lips. She put the meat in her mouth and chewed. Then she moaned, and I had to look away.

"Wow, this is so good. How did you learn to grill? You mentioned that you grew up in the city; there aren't a lot of options here for people to grill."

"My sister's place had a patio area with a grill. Her husband showed me the basics, and I taught myself the rest."

"That's pretty cool. You're really, really good at it."

I ducked my head, not used to the praise. "Thank you. I enjoy it."

She took another bite and moaned again. I wished she'd stop making that sound. "It's a shame you want to be a journalist because you are so good at grilling."

I laughed. "I have a split passion. My ideal position would be writing about food."

"Like a critic?"

I shook my head and grimaced. "Oh man, no way. I would hate that job. Have people fear you and hate you, but fall at your feet anyway? That sounds terrible."

"I bet it's one hell of a power trip, though," she laughed.

I nodded. "Probably."

"So, what is it about food that you want to write about?"

She seemed to be genuinely interested, so I told her. "Ideally, I'd like to have a column about grilling or something like that. Maybe feature a different recipe or technique in each issue, or have a Q and A. I don't know, the idea isn't fully formed," I said, feeling like an idiot for sharing a half-baked idea with her. She seemed so put together, and I felt like I was missing pieces.

"I think that's a great idea. *You're the Man* doesn't have anything like that and most men's magazines have some kind of food feature."

"Yeah, but I'd have to get it through Roger first." And therein laid the problem. *Roger*. The cockblocker of dreams. I would have loved to be able to do a column right there at *You're the Man* since I was familiar with the staff and the way the magazine was published. But I doubted Roger would ever see me as anything other than his assistant.

Melanie made a face, probably coming to the same conclusion as me. She was a smart girl. "Well, if you write anything like you cook, he wouldn't be able to turn you down."

She was good for my ego. "What about you?" I asked, feeling uncomfortable with all the talk being focused on me.

"What about me?"

"What are your grand plans for life after *Leading Lady*?" Pink spread across her cheeks again; she didn't like to be the center of attention either. She seemed to be weighing whether or not to answer me. I hoped she did.

"I design clothes," she finally answered. "I want to have my own fashion line."

- 8 -
Melanie

I let the words linger in the air between us. Usually when I told guys my career aspirations, they thought it was a joke…or they made a joke out of it. I wasn't sure why being a fashion designer seemed so silly to some people. It was a perfectly respectable career, look at Donna Karan or Alexander McQueen. Or Marc Jacobs or Tom Ford or Karl Lagerfeld. I didn't delude myself into thinking I'd reach their level, but nothing was impossible.

I just had to try…

"That's pretty cool," Tyler said, and I relaxed. "What kinds of things do you design?"

"Right now, I'm just focusing on women's clothes. I make some of the things I wear," I said, gesturing to my outfit. It was another sundress, this one was dark blue with a contrasting dark pink neckline and halter top.

"Wow, you designed that? And sewed it?" He asked, surprised.

"Yep. I've probably designed most of the outfits you've seen me in."

"That's pretty awesome. I'd ask you to make me something, but I don't know what."

I laughed. "I'll see if I can come up with something. I started with women's clothes because that's what attracted me to fashion when I was little, plus I could use myself to model it."

"Well, you do a great job modeling it, Spice." He was smirking at me, and it made my face heat up. I was probably bright red. That was also not the first time he called me Spice and I wondered why I'd earned the nickname.

"Why do you call me that?"

He looked away, then looked back. "It's nothing bad, I swear. But can I tell you later?"

"No, now I'm even more intrigued."

He sighed. "Your name…Melanie…there are two Spice Girls named Melanie."

"So, you call me *Spice* because of the Spice Girls?" He nodded, and I could tell he was embarrassed. It was pretty funny, but I wouldn't laugh at him. "My best friend is getting married and asked me to design and make her wedding dress." I wasn't sure why I shared that piece of information with him, but I did. I figured I owed him something after the whole *Spice* thing...like a subject change…and when I was with him, the words just seemed to flow.

"That's awesome. I bet it's difficult though."

I nodded. "It can be difficult to make a wedding dress. Some designs have such intricate details that need to be hand stitched. Meredith — that's my friend — she likes simple designs, so her dress won't be as detailed, but the silk and lace fabrics are so delicate that I have to be careful. Doing something too fast can damage the fabric and cause me to have to restart the whole thing."

"Wow, sort of makes me appreciate the *undo* button in Word documents."

I laughed. "Yeah, it sort of does. I wish I had an *undo* button sometimes."

"Make a lot of bad choices?" he asked, and my eyes shot up from my plate to him. He was smiling, making a joke.

"I meant on my designs," I said, returning his smile. "But it could be cool to have an *undo* button for life stuff. Nothing major, of course, but for the little things? Like being able to undo sleeping through an alarm or answering the phone."

"Missing the train," he suggested.

"Yes! Or burning dinner."

His eyes narrowed. "Is something burnt?"

"Not at all. Everything is great. What seasoning did you use on the vegetables?"

"If I told you, I'd have to kill you." He had a drop-dead serious expression on his face, which made me laugh.

"Ah," I said. "A trade secret. I completely understand. I've got some of those, too."

He raised an eyebrow. "Secret stitches?"

I laughed. "I suppose. But mostly at the magazine."

"What's it like working for Brianna Heatherly? Is she as horrible a boss as Roger?"

I shook my head. "No, not at all. Brianna is a wonderful boss. She's tough, but that's why she's the best. She doesn't take any crap, and she doesn't put up with crap either. She's well respected at the magazine and in the industry."

"She's got that advantage over Roger then. I don't think anyone at the magazine respects him."

"I'm surprised he still has a job, honestly. Preston Parks doesn't usually mess around with stuff like that. It's why Brianna keeps everything so structured at *LL*." Tyler looked like he wanted to say something, but he stopped himself. "I'm sorry for bad mouthing your boss…"

"Don't worry about it," he said, taking a sip of beer. "I can't stand the guy. You can say anything you want about him."

"I'd rather talk about something else," I said, hoping we could talk about something other than work. "I listened to the tape."

His eyes lit up. "Oh yeah? What did you think?"

I took another sip of my beer. The condensation made my hand wet, and I took my time drying it with a napkin. I was making him sweat and enjoying it.

"It was okay…"

"Just okay?" he asked, leaning back in his seat.

I grinned at him. "Better than okay," I said. "I really liked it. I'd forgotten about a few of those songs."

"Ha! I told you." He said looking all proud of himself.

"Hey, now. I just said I liked the tape. I didn't say it was better than the eighties."

He narrowed his eyes at me. "We're not supposed to talk about decades."

"You're right, we're not." We'd agreed to that after our disastrous lunch date. "But first, do you have Spotify?"

"Yeah," he said, drawing the word out.

"I made an eighties playlist for you."

"I guess I'll check it out since you listened to my tape."

I made a face at him. "Thanks for your sacrifice."

"Anytime." He smirked.

We spent another hour talking about where we

went to college, our favorite Manhattan restaurants, and what we liked about the city. It was surprising how much we had in common, and the conversation between us flowed easily. When some other people came up to use the grill, I helped him gather everything up and bring it back down to his apartment where he had cookies and milk for dessert. He seemed almost embarrassed by it, but I thought it was adorable. We sat on the futon—which doubled as his bed—and ate our dessert while having a surprisingly tame debate over which was the better of the two: cheesecake or carrot cake.

"I'd like to walk you home," he said at the end of the night. We could have continued talking for the rest of the night, I thought, but we both had to work in the morning, and I couldn't stop yawning.

"That would be really nice," I agreed.

We only lived a few blocks from each other; we both chose tiny apartments close to our office building since our jobs often demanded so much of our time. For what we were paying for our tiny apartments, we could probably rent something spacious outside of the city, but who wanted to do that? Manhattan was an amazing place to live. He held my hand the entire way home, even in the elevator. I felt like I'd floated home on a cloud, just being with Tyler gave me a natural high. He'd given me a kiss on the cheek when he left me at my apartment after our escape room date, and I was hoping that tonight he'd give me a little more than that. I wasn't ready to sleep with him, but a good kiss would have been a great way to end an amazing night.

We paused outside my apartment door, and I

thought about inviting him in, but I didn't say the words.

"I had a really great time tonight, Melanie." He stood just inches from me, looking into my eyes.

"Me too," I said, meeting his gaze. "Thank you for dinner."

"You're welcome. I'm glad you liked it."

"It was delicious." Okay, this was getting awkward. Were we just going to exchange pleasantries?

"When can I see you again?"

"Any time you want."

He smiled.

I smiled.

He leaned in.

I leaned in.

Our lips met.

My body lit up.

I wrapped my arms around his neck as he pressed me against my apartment door. He licked the seam of my lips, and I opened for him. I tasted his mouth, still tasting faintly of beer and something sweet…cookies. He was pulling away before I was ready for him to, taking the warm solidness of his body away from mine.

He rested his head against mine and sighed. "If I don't leave now, I might never go, and we should both get some sleep tonight."

The mental imagery I got from the promise of those words…

He was right, though. It had already been closing in on midnight when we'd left his apartment.

"I'll talk to you tomorrow?" he asked.

"Definitely."

"Good night, Spice," he winked. Then he landed a quick peck on my lips and turned away.

"Good night, Tyler." I let myself into my apartment, closed the door behind me, and leaned against it.

If I wasn't careful, I was going to fall for that man.

Tyler: What are you up to?

Melanie: You know I'm working…

Tyler: Yeah…

Melanie: Are you bored?

Tyler: Yes!! Want to entertain me?

Melanie: Wish I could but Brianna has a deadline.

Tyler: Where is your desk?

Melanie: In front of Brianna's office??

Tyler: I mean where on the floor. Like when you get off the elevator, where do you go?

Melanie: Straight back, then to the left. Why?

Melanie: Wait! You can't come here!! The last person whose boyfriend came and visited them at work got fired!

Melanie: And I didn't say that meaning you are my boyfriend…just that you are my friend, who is a boy, and the semantics won't matter to Brianna.

Tyler: I don't want to visit you at work. Jeez, calm down. I was just wondering if our floors were laid out in the same way. I could be on top of you right now.

Melanie: What?

Tyler: That came out wrong.

Tyler: Sorry.

Tyler: So, do you want to be my girlfriend?

Melanie: We've only had 2 dates.

Tyler: We've had 3 dates, we're just choosing to discount one of them.

Melanie: Are you seriously asking me to be your girlfriend? Like we're in high school or something? Do people our age even do that anymore.

Tyler: Sorry, do you want to go steady?

Melanie: …

Tyler: What does that mean?

Tyler: What does … mean?

Tyler: Melanie?

Tyler: Spice…

Melanie: Sorry, Brianna had to speak to me.

Tyler: Did I get you fired?

Melanie: No.

Tyler: Good. Now, look. I don't know what people our age say to indicate that they want to date someone exclusively. But I want to. Date you, and only you. So what do you say?

Tyler: Wanna feel my shirt? It's made of boyfriend material. ;)

Melanie: OMG you're a dork.

Tyler: I can't believe you just used OMG. I retract my question.

Tyler: Just kidding, I don't.

Tyler: Date me, please?

Melanie: Yes.

Tyler: Yeah?

Melanie: Yes, I will be your girlfriend.

Melanie: But, for the record, I cannot believe you asked me to be your girlfriend via text.

Tyler: Oh, come on. Give me a break. It's not like I proposed via text.

Melanie: If you propose to me via text, I'm saying no.

Melanie: Not that you're going to propose to me.

Melanie: Like ever.

Tyler: You're adorable.

Tyler: Melanie? Where did you go?

Tyler: Mel?

Melanie: Who is this?

Tyler: Apparently the future Mr… What's your last name?

Tyler: Mel?

Tyler: Was that too soon?

Tyler: I'm sorry.

Tyler: Can you at least send me a … so I know you don't completely hate me.

Melanie: …

Tyler: Ah, thank you. I'd hate to break up five seconds after making it official. I didn't even get a chance to change my relationship status on Facebook yet.

***

Melanie: You never told me! Did you like the playlist?

Tyler: I haven't listened to it yet.

Melanie: What?

Tyler: Sorry, been busy.

Melanie: You're such a liar. You told me at lunch yesterday that you counted all the fluorescent lights on your floor.

Tyler: That wasn't me. That was Pete. Pete counted all the fluorescent lights. He wanted me to help, but I told him I was too busy. You must have misunderstood.

Melanie: …

Tyler: Are we back to that?

Melanie: …

Tyler: At least you're still texting me.

Tyler: Melanie?

Tyler: Mel?

***

Tyler: I listened to the playlist.

Melanie: Did you like it?
Tyler: Just kidding! Gotcha!
Tyler: Mel?
Tyler: Come on…
Tyler: Fine…

***

Tyler: OK, it wasn't so bad. The Beastie Boys are cool. They have some decent 90s music, too.
Melanie: So you listened to my eighties playlist and the only thing you got from it was that the Beastie Boys also had songs in the 90s?
Tyler: Journey is cool, too. That song was on Glee.
Melanie: …
Tyler: Some of the chick songs were OK.
Melanie: …
Tyler: This is why we weren't supposed to talk about this stuff. We talk about music and I get the dots. I don't want the dots.
Melanie: I gave your stuff a chance, Tyler.
*Tyler: *sigh**
Melanie: Really? You are so dramatic.
Tyler: OK. I will do another listen.
Melanie: Thank you. I appreciate that.
Tyler: I'm always willing to compromise. And by compromise, I mean do whatever you tell me to do.
Melanie: What do you want?
Tyler: What do you mean?
Melanie: You're after something…you don't do whatever I tell you to do.
Tyler: I do so.
Melanie: No, you don't. The other night, after we watched Golden Girls, *every time you said something to me, you prefaced it with "picture it."*
Tyler: So I've adopted Sophia's style of storytelling,

what do you have against her?
Melanie: …
Tyler: Fine. My sister invited us to dinner on
Saturday. Will you come?
Melanie: I'd love to. That's so sweet of her. Can I
bring something?
Tyler: Just your beautiful self.
Melanie: *blushing*
Tyler: I like making you blush.

***

Tyler: That Roxette song was in Pretty Woman*!*
Melanie: Yes, it was.
Tyler: That was a 90s movie.
Melanie: The song was released in the 80s.
Tyler: Were you even alive in the 80s? Shouldn't
you prefer the 90s by default?
Melanie: That's irrelevant.
Tyler: I think it's a pretty good argument.
Tyler: Don't give me the dots. Please.
Melanie: What do you want to do tonight?
Tyler: Watch TV
Melanie: What should we watch?
Tyler: Does it really matter?
Melanie: Of course it matters. I think we should
finish Saved by the Bell.
Tyler: Whatever. We're just going to end up making
out, anyway.
Melanie: Maybe we won't.
Tyler: What do you mean?
Melanie: Maybe we'll actually watch the show.
Tyler: Um. My TV is broken.
Melanie: It wasn't last night.
Tyler: It fell off the wall this morning.
Melanie: …

Tyler: I canceled my Hulu subscription.
Melanie: We can use mine.
Tyler: You don't have one.
Melanie: I just subscribed. Just now. I downloaded the app and subscribed.
Tyler: You are such a dirty liar.
*Melanie: *shrugs**
Tyler: Fine. We can watch Saved by the Bell.
Melanie: Thanks, babe. Way to compromise. ;)
Tyler: Told you…

***

Melanie: Are you sure I can't bring something to your sister's house?
Melanie: Dessert or something?
Tyler: No.
Melanie: I can bake something. I make really great oatmeal cookies.
Tyler: Oatmeal doesn't belong in cookies.
Melanie: Excuse me?
Tyler: Oatmeal cookies would be lovely, but you don't have an oven.
Melanie: I can use the communal kitchen.
Tyler: Do you have cookie sheets?
Melanie: Well, no. But I have aluminum foil and I can wrap the communal cookie sheet in that.
Tyler: …
Melanie: Don't you dot me.
Tyler: You don't get to have all the fun.
Tyler: …
Tyler: …
Tyler: …
Melanie: That's not the way this works. That's not the way any of this works.
Melanie: …

Tyler: I'll see you in 2 hours. Just settle down. Hannah is going to love you. You don't have to be or bring anything but yourself.

Melanie: *swoon*

Tyler: *brushes off shoulders* My work here is done.

Melanie: *rolls eyes* I love how modest you are.

Tyler: It's my best quality.

Melanie: I wouldn't say that.

Tyler: What?

Melanie: I'll see you at 5!

Tyler: smh

- 10 -
Melanie

"I'm *so* sorry, Tyler. I feel awful."

"Stop apologizing. It's not your fault."

"But we're going to be *late*, and it is *my* fault!"

"Your boss called with a legit emergency. That's not your fault."

"I'm not so sure I'd call it an emergency," I grumbled.

"She was in a car accident…"

I let out a sigh. "I know, and I'm glad that she's safe. I'm just upset that it had to happen right when I'm meeting your family for the first time. I must seem like a complete tart."

He laughed at me. *Laughed!* "My sister doesn't think you're a tart. Trust me. She's totally cool with it, and we're only thirty minutes behind schedule. We're *fashionably late*. See what I did there?" he asked, wriggling his eyebrows.

"You're such a dork," I said, rising to my tiptoes to kiss his scruffy cheek. "Are you sure it's okay?"

He kissed the tip of my nose as we strolled side by side, my arm wrapped around his firm bicep. "I'm positive. Dinner is not until six. We planned for five so we could have cocktails, but it's really not a big deal."

"If you say so."

We'd been dating exclusively for about a month

and everything was going great. Aside from our difference in opinion about music, we had a lot in common and got along well. We compromised when it came to television and movies, which helped when it came to our at-home date nights, which were becoming increasingly more frequent. Simply put: we couldn't get enough of each other. We hadn't slept together yet, but things between us were getting hot and heavy and I knew that next step was right around the corner. Maybe tonight if I played my cards right…

"Here we are," he said as we approached a brick high rise on Park Avenue. His sister and her husband must have been loaded. He hadn't mentioned their wealth before. Suddenly, I felt more nervous. He stepped forward, but I stayed still. "Hey, what's going on?" he asked, stopping outside the door and turning to face me.

"Your sister lives on Park Avenue?"

He shrugged. "Yeah. Is that a problem?"

I shook my head. "No. I just wish I'd known." I looked down at my black pencil skirt and royal blue scoop neck blouse combo and felt like I was naked. His sister probably wore Chanel and Louboutin and there I was in my Melanie Katsaros original. *Gah!*

"And what difference would it have made?" he asked, running his hands up and down my bare arms.

"I don't know."

"You would have been stuck in your head about it a lot earlier, right?" I nodded. We really had been spending a lot of time together. He knew me too well. "Didn't I tell you she was going to love you?"

"Yes, like a thousand times."

"So it shouldn't matter how much money is in their bank account, right?"

"Right."

"You ready?"

"Yeah. Thanks for the pep talk."

"Any time."

He took my hand and pulled me through into the building, nodding at the suited doorman who held open the large door for us.

"Mr. Scott," the doorman said.

"James," Tyler returned.

My eyes went wide as I took in the white marble lobby. I'd momentarily forgotten that Tyler had moved in with his sister and her husband after his parents died. He *lived* in this kind of luxury at one point in time. We stepped onto a gold elevator and a man in a suit identical to the doorman pressed the button for the penthouse.

Ohmygod.

"Relax," Tyler said, turning his head and kissing my hair.

I cleared my throat and released the iron grip I had on his hand. "Sorry."

The elevator bell dinged and the doors opened to a stark white hallway with black marble floors. Tyler tugged my hand again, leading me off the elevator and towards the double doors at the end of the short hallway. We were about ten feet away when the doors opened and a beautiful woman with Tyler's blue eyes appeared, smiling at us.

"Ty!" she said, pulling Tyler in for a hug.

"Han," he greeted. "This is Melanie. Mel, this is my sister, Hannah."

"It's so great to finally meet you!" Hannah said,

surprising me by pulling me in for a hug. "Tyler has been talking about you non-stop. I feel like I already know you."

"It's nice to meet you, too," I said when she released me.

"She's more gorgeous than you let on, Ty," she said.

"Jesus, Han. Lay off."

"Am I being too much?" she asked, giving me a wink. Tyler was blushing now, and I knew she was teasing him. "It's just that he's never brought a girl home before. There are years of pent up big-sistering I have to get out."

"That's not a thing," Tyler said.

"It's not?" she asked.

"I definitely think it *is* a thing," I contributed.

Tyler scowled at me. "You're on my side."

"Am I?"

He narrowed his eyes. "Yes. You two have just met, you don't get to start ganging up on me in the doorway. At least wait until after dinner."

"Okay. Truce," Hannah offered.

Tyler put his palm on my lower back and guided me farther into the penthouse. *Penthouse.* There was so much to take in. Everything appeared so clean and white, but also homey, in a strange way. Tyler guided us into a room to the left of the front hall, it appeared to be a lounge of some kind. There were a couple of loveseats facing each other, and a small bar in the corner.

"Beer or wine?" Tyler asked me.

"White wine would be nice." I preferred beer over wine, but the occasion seemed more appropriate for wine. Tyler gave me a questioning look, and I smiled and nodded.

"Where's Pres?" he asked Hannah. I guessed that was her husband.

"He's in his office. Work emergency." She smiled apologetically. "He'll be down in a few."

Tyler brought me and his sister glasses of wine, then returned to the bar to pour his drink. I sat down on one of the loveseats, his sister sat on the other, and Tyler sat beside me with a short glass of amber liquid. Whiskey, perhaps?

"So, Melanie. Tyler tells me you're a fashion designer."

I turned my wide eyes to Tyler. "Embellish much?" I whispered. Not quietly enough though, because Hannah laughed. "I just play around…"

"She doesn't play around," Tyler said. "She designs a lot of what she wears, and she's working on a wedding dress for her friend."

Hannah's eyes lit up. "A wedding dress? Really? Wow…I always used to doodle dresses and stuff when I was younger, but I never dreamed of designing something that could actually become something, you know?"

Oddly, I knew exactly what she meant. "Yes, I started the same way. Then I started going to thrift stores and craft stores with my allowance and the money I made from babysitting and creating things based off my drawings."

"Wow, that's so cool. Are all of your designs repurposed thrift store finds?"

"No, none actually. That was my direction in high school but once I got to college and took some design classes, I fell in love with boho-chic. I'm actually working on a line that's sort of conservative boho-chic. I really wanted to design something that could pass as professional work wear."

"That's very cool. Did you design what you're wearing now?"

"The top, yes." I held my arms out to the side so she could see the how the fabric fell around my waist. "It looks like it's tucked into the skirt, right? But it's not."

"Wow, that's so cool. I wish I could commission a few pieces from you. I love your style."

My face heated. I wasn't used to being complimented on my designs since generally no one ever knew they were mine. "Thank you."

"Of course!" Hannah smiled.

We spent the next few minutes talking about our favorite designers and the best places to shop. Tyler inserted the occasional comment, but mainly left Hannah and I to speak in a language he didn't quite understand. He'd said as much.

By the time Hannah's husband made his appearance, I had a pretty good idea of what designs in my closet Hannah would like. Maybe I'd bring something over one day...

- 11 -
Tyler

Melanie and my sister were hitting it off better than I'd ever expected. I was glad to see her so relaxed considering how tense she'd been on the way over. I had planned on taking an Uber, but when I was waiting for her to finish her work emergency, I knew she'd need the walk to calm down. I was hoping the wine and conversation would have her so laid back that she wouldn't get pissed at me for what was about to happen. For not being completely honest with her...

"Preston! There you are. Come meet Melanie," Hannah said, looking behind me and Melanie.

Showtime.

Melanie and I stood, turning to face my brother-in-law together. I heard Melanie's gasp as I stepped forward and gave him a bro hug.

"Melanie, good to see you again," Preston said, smiling at my frozen girlfriend. I nudged her with my elbow.

"Mr. Parks, it's good to see you, too." She held out her hand, and he took it.

"Call me Preston, please. I hate being called Mr. Parks, even at the office."

"Preston," Melanie said, trying the word out. The two syllables rolling awkwardly off her tongue.

Preston smiled. "What have you got there, Ty?"

"Whiskey, neat."

"Macallan?"

"Glenfiddich."

Preston laughed. "Always after the best?" I smirked, knowing he was going to try to make me look bad. "Melanie, this clown you're dating threw a huge party his senior year of high school when his sister and I were out of town for business. They drank all my liquor, expensive shit, too. I think one of the bottles was over twenty thousand dollars."

Melanie looked at me, still wide-eyed. "Twenty thousand dollars?" she asked no one in particular.

Preston nodded. "Yeah. The little shit puked it all up the next day, too. We got a call from our housekeeper the next morning, and Hannah had to come home early to take care of him."

"I didn't mind," Hannah said. Whenever she had to do something maternal for me, she always added the disclaimer that she didn't mind, so I wouldn't think I was a burden, even though I knew she was really pissed that time. She could say it as often as she wanted, but I still knew it wasn't exactly convenient for her to have to take care of her younger brother when she was still basically a child herself. She should have been enjoying being a newlywed instead of becoming an insta-mom to her ornery teenage brother.

"Anyway," Preston said, taking a seat beside Hannah and placing a kiss on the side of her head. She closed her eyes at the contact and smiled. My sister hit the lottery with Preston Parks, literally and figuratively. So had I. "I'm guessing the work emergency that held you up, Melanie, was the same one that held me up."

"Oh, I guess it was. I'm glad Brianna wasn't hurt."

"The woman works too hard," Preston said.

"She does. It's why she's the best."

"Indeed. She speaks very highly of you."

"Oh, um…"

Preston laughed lightly. "Don't worry. She doesn't know you're dating my brother-in-law." Melanie looked relieved, and I wasn't sure how I felt about that. "Tyler here keeps his professional life and his personal life completely separate; I assume you'd want to do the same."

She looked at me, then back at Preston. "Yes, please."

"Not a problem. What's for dinner, Han?"

While my sister went into a lengthy description of the menu, I placed my hand on Melanie's leg, just above her knee. She then crossed her legs, letting my hand fall to the sofa cushion. She glanced at me briefly, and I knew what she was saying.

"…"

***

"I can't believe you didn't tell me Preston Parks is your brother-in-law!"

I ignored the scalding tone of Melanie's voice, instead opting to appreciate the fact that she was finally talking to me again. We had a nice dinner with Hannah and Preston. She spoke to the two of them at length about this, that, and the other thing, but she only spoke directly to me when absolutely necessary. It did not go unnoticed by Hannah, who whispered in my ear when I was hugging her goodbye that I should have told her about Preston.

I took Melanie's coat from her and hung it on the hook on the back of my apartment door. I was surprised she even came back to my apartment with me, though I'm not entirely sure she realized she had since she silently fumed the entire way here.

"I don't typically share that information because of work."

"But we're dating, Tyler. I understand why you might not want to share that information with a coworker, but I'm your girlfriend."

"I'm sorry."

"You should be. You completely blindsided me. I was feeling bad enough being late, and then having that bomb dropped on me? How embarrassing. Everyone knew but me. I just saw Preston last week and he said nothing, but he knew, didn't he? He knew I was your girlfriend?"

I nodded, feeling a little ashamed, but not much. I still didn't think it was a big deal, but I understood why she did.

She flopped down on my bed and kicked off her shoes. "I'm so mad at you."

"I know," I said, kicking off my shoes.

"Like really mad."

"I know you are," I said as I unbuttoned my shirt. She eyed my fingers as they released each button. "I'm sorry." I tossed my shirt in the laundry basket on the floor of my closet.

"Hmm?" She was staring at my naked chest.

"I said I was sorry."

She looked up at me, snapping out of her lust induced haze. "Why didn't you tell me?"

"It just didn't come up. Honestly. I didn't think

about it until Hannah invited us to dinner and I realized you'd recognize him. I wasn't intentionally keeping it from you. I don't volunteer the information because he owns the company. He took it over when his father retired a few years ago. I got my job on my own merit, and I don't want people to assume I got it handed to me because Preston is family."

"I never would have thought that about you."

"I know, babe. But other people would." I unbuttoned my slacks and they dropped to the floor. Melanie was once again distracted. I walked over to my dresser and pulled out a t-shirt, tossing it at her.

"What's this for?"

"You're sleeping over."

"I am?"

"Yep."

She stood up from her place on the bed and I thought she'd make a move to leave, but she didn't. Instead she pulled her blouse over her head, tossing it on the loveseat. Standing in front of me in her black skirt and a black lace bra, beautiful wasn't enough of a word to describe the sight. Neither was breathtaking. Melanie was all those things and more. She reached behind her and unzipped her skirt. It fell to the floor revealing a black lace thong that matched her bra. She kicked her skirt off her feet, and it landed next to my pants. I liked seeing our discarded clothing next to each other on the floor like that.

I looked back to Melanie and she took a step towards me. There was heat in her eyes, probably the same heat that was in my eyes.

Another step.

That was all it took.

- 12 -
Melanie

Tyler and I were a mess of lips and hands and tongues.

His hands went straight for my shoulders, sliding the straps of my bra down my arms. My hands felt up his pecs and down the ridges of his abs. He worked out a lot, and I loved feeling the hot benefits under my fingertips. Our mouths were fused together, breathing each other in and tasting each other's wants. With a groan, Tyler pushed me back so I landed on his bed. He crawled over me, and his forearms framed my face as he looked into my eyes.

"Are you sure you want to do this?" he asked.

I nodded.

"Say the words, Melanie," he demanded. His voice was rough, full of need. Need for me. I'd never felt so powerful.

"Yes, I want this, Tyler. I need you." I emphasized my point by lifting my hips to meet his. I let out a small moan when my sensitive parts met his very hard parts.

He kissed me again, then rose to his knees. He was still straddling my legs when he pulled me up so I was sitting flush against him, then he reached his hands around my back to unclasp my bra. He pulled it off, tossing it onto our growing clothes pile on the floor. He pushed me back down onto the bed and looked down at me for a moment. I about came out of my skin when he reached his hand into his boxer briefs and squeezed.

"I want to fuck you so bad."

"What are you waiting for?" I asked, grabbing the backs of his strong thighs and pulling him back down on top of me. I loved the feel of his weight on me, the pressure…

Tyler kissed me as he ran his hands down to my hips and pushed my panties down. I helped wriggle them the rest of the way off. Then I did the same with his boxers, feeling the length of him hit my upper thigh as he kicked his shorts off each foot. It was big and heavy, and I couldn't wait to feel it inside me. Tyler ran a finger through my wet center, and I spread my legs, letting him know I was more than ready for him. I rocked my hips as he dipped and rubbed, teasing me to the point of squirming.

"Please, Tyler."

He let out a dark chuckle before reaching for the drawer of his nightstand. He ripped the foil wrapper open with his teeth. I laughed as he spit out the piece he'd torn off, but my humor quickly turned to desire as I watched him roll the condom on. God, he was beautiful.

He moved back down and kissed me, one hand holding my breast while the other hand lined him up with my opening. I gasped when he pressed inside, feeling every single inch of him.

"Mel, you're so tight."

"You feel so good," I told him, rocking my hips against him. I lifted myself up and nipped at his chest, kissing and licking him playfully, trying to get to his nipple. He tasted salty, like fresh sweat and something sweeter. He groaned and began pumping himself in and out at a steady pace, causing me to fall back onto the bed. He kissed my mouth, nipped my earlobe, then licked his way down to my breasts. He paid each nipple proper attention before returning to my mouth where he picked up the pace. "Oh, Tyler!"

"Do you like that?" he asked when his thumb found my clit, moving in a circular motion that was dizzying.

"Yes," I panted. "I'm going to come. Don't stop. Please, don't stop." He leaned in and kissed me again as he pumped harder. I called out his name as a series of tiny explosions burst from within me. My body radiated pleasure from my center all the way out to my curled toes and clenched fists. I saw stars behind my eyelids as I vibrated with my release.

His pace quickened even more before he let out a feral grow and jerked inside of me as he came. He collapsed on top of me, our sweaty messy bodies sticking to each other as we kissed, coming down from the ultimate high we'd just experienced.

"It's never been *that* good," I confessed, speaking of the orgasm that nearly blacked me out.

"For me, either," he said, his voice muffled since his face was in the pillow over my shoulder. I laughed and pushed him off me. He got up and discarded the condom and wrapper in his small bathroom. Then he returned, lying down beside me. I snuggled up against him and closed my eyes.

***

"Wait," I said, holding up my hand. We were lying on our backs on Tyler's bed, our heads sharing a pillow and our legs tangled up in the sheets after round two. The sheets were damp with our sweat and the room held the musty scent of sex. We were in the middle of a deep discussion about the benefits of late-night Chinese delivery when something occurred to me. "Why haven't you ever told Preston what a shit Roger is?"

"I keep my professional life and my personal life separate."

I lifted my head and looked at him, a confused expression on my face. "But he makes your work life miserable, and he doesn't do his job. *You* do his job." He'd confessed that to me weeks ago after he'd had an awful day at work. I couldn't believe that Roger got away with even more than the rumors had let on.

"He'll get what's coming to him eventually."

"But someone needs to turn him in for that to happen, and you're in the best position to do that."

"I'm not a rat, Mel. The last thing I need is to go running to Preston to tell on my boss. That kind of thing would spread through our industry like wildfire. I'd *never* earn a writing job with that on my resume."

"Don't think of it as being a rat, Tyler. It's your brother-in-law's business and Roger is giving the magazine a bad name. Surely people in the industry would understand, no one likes Roger. You'd probably get job offers." It wasn't even a lie; people would probably praise Tyler for getting rid of Roger. I know Brianna would.

"Preston knows Roger is a dick."

"Then why doesn't he get rid of him?"

"It's not that easy, I guess."

"Because he's so good at his job? The one you do for him? Preston doesn't know that, does he?" I didn't know Preston Parks well, but from what little I did know, he wouldn't tolerate Roger taking credit for someone else's work, whether that person was his brother-in-law or not.

"Look, I'd really rather not be talking about Roger or Preston right now. Can we just bask in the afterglow and enjoy this moment?"

I sighed, knowing he was right. I was ruining our post-coital moment. "Yes, of course. I'm sorry."

He pulled me into his side, and I rested my head on his chest. He kissed the top of my head. "Tonight was amazing, Melanie. Thank you."

"Thank *you*, Ty."

"Go to bed," he kissed my head again and I closed my eyes, instantly falling asleep.

- 13 -
Tyler

I hate my job. I hate my job. I hate my job.

I was sitting in a meeting, taking notes, listening to Roger blast the advertising department for their lack of productivity. Roger. Talking. About. Lack. Of. Productivity. I could count on one hand — one finger — the amount of times Roger has actually done Roger's job. He had some audacity.

"Did you get all that, Scott?"

Patronizing mother fu-

"Yes, Mr. Hoffstadt." I was jotting down the names of the five people he just put on warning. In front of all the other departments.

"Now, if you could all be as productive as Scott here."

"His name is Tyler."

Oh...no he didn't. Poor Joe. Poor, dumb Joe. He was a new hire, worked in the mailroom. While I appreciated him having my back, he had no idea what he'd just got himself into. You didn't correct Roger. You just didn't. It wasn't worth it. If Roger wanted to call me Bob, I'd let him call me Bob.

"Excuse me?" Roger glared at Joe.

Joe shifted in his seat and looked at me. I gave a quick shake of my head that Roger couldn't see. Then he looked at Roger. "I said," he cleared his throat, "I thought his name was Tyler."

I rolled my eyes. *Shouldn't have said anything, Joe.*

"What does it matter to you what I call him?" Roger asked Joe, hooking his thumb at me.

"N-nothing, sir."

"That's what I thought." Roger looked down at the agenda on the conference table. He probably would have fired Joe, but I didn't think he knew who he was. "If no one else has anything to add, this meeting is adjourned."

Everyone smartly said nothing, just collected their things and left the room. I stayed behind, straightening up the room so the next group who came in didn't have a mess. That, and I knew if I waited long enough, Roger would be gone by the time I returned to my desk.

"What an asshole, huh?" I looked up. It was Joe.

I looked around, making sure the coast was clear before I nodded. "I appreciate what you said in there, but it's not worth it. The best way to get by working here is to keep your head down and do your job."

Joe nodded. "Thanks for the tip. Want to grab some lunch?"

I looked at my watch. "I can't, I'm meeting my girlfriend." He looked dejected. It sucked being the new guy, especially in a field dominated by women. Sure, *You're the Man* was a men's magazine, but there were still more women than men behind the scenes. "Maybe tomorrow?"

"That would be cool."

Joe helped me straighten the rest of the chairs around the large, oak conference room table. I dumped a few coffee cups in the trash, turned off the light, and said goodbye to Joe. I had a date to get to.

***

Across the table, Melanie picked at her salad. She moved the lettuce, tomatoes, and chicken around her plate, but didn't take any bites.

The salad should have been my first clue something was wrong. My girl didn't eat salads. She wasn't afraid to eat real food. The second or third time we hung out, we went slice for slice on an eighteen inch pepperoni pizza. She had no shame about it either, not that she should have. I thought it was awesome. A woman who actually ate...much better than some of the women I'd dated before, especially for one who worked in the fashion industry. Those women usually ate like birds, trying to fit into the latest designer outfit.

"All right," I said, finally breaking the silence. Her head popped up, her big hazel eyes focused on me. "What's going on?"

"What do you mean?" I raised my eyebrows and she sighed. She was caught and she knew it. "I'm sorry, I guess I'm a little nervous."

"Why?" What could she have to be nervous about? We'd only been dating a short time, but we shared pretty much everything with one another. We kept no secrets.

She shifted in her seat, nervously looking around the restaurant. Was she going to break up with me?

"Mel?" My voice actually cracked a little.

She sighed. "My parents are having a party this weekend. I was wondering if you'd like to come."

She practically mumbled the last sentence, so I leaned forward and asked her to repeat herself. "I was wondering if you'd like to come."

I took a relieved breath. "Why would you be nervous to ask me that?" She shrugged, looking back at her salad. "Babe," I said, reaching across the table and lifting her chin until her eyes met mine. "You have nothing to be nervous about. You've already met my family."

"Yeah, but your family is normal. Mine is not." I raised an eyebrow. My family was *far* from normal. She rolled her eyes. "I'm not talking about the structure of my family tree, Tyler. I'm talking about behavior. Have you ever seen *My Big Fat Greek Wedding?*"

"Yeah, that's the one with the guy from *Sex and the City* in it." Now it was her turn to raise a brow. "I have an older sister," I sighed.

"Uh huh. Somehow I think your knowledge of *Sex and the City* has more to do with your nineties obsession than your sister."

"It started in 1998, most of it was in the 2000s. That doesn't exactly qualify-"

"The fact that you know the year it began is alarming," she deadpanned.

"We're getting off track," I said, knowing I'd pretty much screwed myself with that one. Yeah, I watched the show. Sexy single women living it up in New York City, what wasn't there to like? *Sue me.*

"The party is probably going to be massive...aunts, uncles, and cousins."

"I'm not afraid of your family, Spice."

"I've never brought anyone home before."

Ah, and there we had it. "What are you more

afraid of? My impression of them, or their impression of me?"

She covered her face with both hands. "I don't even know. I love my family and I lo-," she looked away. *What was she about to say?* "I really like you. I'm not embarrassed about either of you, but my family may do something embarrassing."

I reached across the table and took her hand. "I'm pretty sure that's what families are meant to do. Don't worry about it, babe. I'm sure it will be fine."

Suddenly, her eyes went wide, and she pulled her hand back. "I am such an ass."

"Huh?"

"Here I am complaining about my family…"

Oh, I knew what direction she was headed in with that. "Don't be sorry you have a family, Mel."

"I just feel bad."

I fucking hated pity. More than anything else. I strongly believed that some of my former girlfriends dated me because they thought I was a project. An orphaned boy who needed love and affection. My sister had given me plenty of love and affection, though. Sure, it was a different kind of love than what I would have gotten from my mother, but I never felt like I was lacking. Once I got over being pissed at the world for my parents' deaths, I was okay.

"Don't," I told her. Maybe too firmly because she startled. I reached for her hand again. "I'm sorry. I just don't want you, of all people, to pity me."

"I don't pity you," she said, but I could tell by the look in her eyes that she at least felt sad for me. I supposed that was okay. Over the last several weeks, I'd learned she had a lot of feelings. Not that there was anything wrong with that. "Even though your pop culture preferences leave a lot to be desired."

"You really want to go there now? We're in public, Spice."

She shrugged. "Maybe you won't cry like a baby when you have an audience."

"I had something in my eye!"

"Right, it had nothing to do with me winning the argument that the New Kids are a better boy band than 'NSync and Backstreet Boys combined." She looked so smug leaning back in her chair with her arms crossed.

I stretched my arms out in front of me, entwined my fingers, and cracked my knuckles, preparing for war. Banter with Melanie was like an aphrodisiac, and I couldn't wait until later tonight. "Let's do this."

- 14 -
Melanie

The toe of my heeled strappy sandal tapped against the floor of the train car as Tyler and I sped down the tracks towards my parents' home in Port Jefferson. He rested his warm hand on my bare knee and the movement stopped. He had that calming effect on me.

Maybe today wouldn't be so bad after all.

I had my man by my side—I had *a man*, period. There was nothing fun being part of a large family and being single. Everyone was always asking "When are you going to settle down with a nice man?" or, my favorite, "You aren't getting any younger." I was in my early twenties, Aunt B, thanks a lot for making me feel like an old maid. At least my arrival with Tyler would keep them off my back. It was times like those when I wished I had siblings to take some of the heat, but alas, I was an only child.

Tyler popped the lid on the Tupperware and ate another chocolate chip cookie. I couldn't even shame him for it since he made the cookies. I didn't have a culinary bone in my body. Something else my family always had a field day with.

"It's going to be fine," Tyler mumbled around the cookie in his mouth. He was careful to catch the loose crumbs in his hand.

"You can't say that. You haven't met them yet."

"Parents love me."

I raised an eyebrow. "Have you ever met a girlfriend's parents?"

He seemed to consider my question, then shook his head. "Nope. Never really had a girlfriend I wanted to take that step with."

And just like that, I was warm all over again. I wrapped my arm around his and leaned into his side, resting my head against the sleeve of his polo shirt. He smelled like fresh linen, but he couldn't tell me what kind of detergent he used since he always sent his laundry out.

We'd unintentionally matched today, him in a pale blue and green striped shirt and khakis and me in a pale green gingham sundress. My white strappy sandals matched the lightweight sweater I brought with me for the ride home since the late summer evening may end up chillier than the warm day. Tyler was in brown loafers. He looked like a sexy prep. I wanted to demand the conductor turn the train around so I could take him back to my tiny apartment and do things to him.

Tyler smirked. "You've got that look in your eyes."

I blinked, hating how my every thought showed on my face. Shrugging, I ignored his comment. "So remember, my Uncle James-"

"Doesn't like to be touched, but his twin brother, David, is a hugger. I can tell the difference between the two of them because David has a full beard and James wishes he did."

I gave his firm stomach a hard pat. "That's not nice."

He rolled his head back and laughed. "Spice, you said your Uncle James has been trying to grow a beard for years but can only manage to get a few patches here and there. Obviously, he wishes he had the beard his brother does."

"Yeah, well he's sensitive about it, so don't say anything."

He rolled his eyes. "As if I'd use your uncles' beards as my icebreakers. I'm more concerned about not being Greek."

I rolled my eyes. "They wouldn't care if you were female. They're just thrilled I'm bringing a date."

"But you said your family was like the one in *My Big Fat Greek Wedding*."

"Yeah, as in *big* and *Greek*. They don't care if we marry other Greeks. Not that you and I are getting married or anything." *Jesus, Melanie!* How embarrassing. "I swear I didn't tell them that."

"Pink is such a cute color on you." Tyler said, kissing my nose.

"Stop it," I said, swatting him away. My cheeks were so flushed, I knew I was more than just pink. I laid my head back on his shoulder, and he ran his fingers through my long hair.

"You know...I'm definitely not ready for marriage." I felt his body shiver as he cringed at the words. "But if I needed to play the role of doting fiancé for one day, I'd totally do it for you."

I closed my eyes as my heart literally melted in my chest. We were having a ridiculous, hypothetical conversation, and I was falling more in love with him with each word he spoke. We hadn't said the words to each other—better yet, I hadn't said them to him. It was too soon, and I'd probably send him running for the hills, but I felt it. Oh, did I feel it. How could I not? He was the sweetest man, and I knew he cared deeply for me. He didn't say the words, but he showed them.

The train screeched to a halt at the station, and I took a deep breath.

Showtime.

I grasped Tyler's hand as we walked down the narrow aisle to the exit. Stepping onto the station platform, the sun warmed my bare shoulders as I looked around for whichever one of my family members drew the short straw to pick me up.

"Wow, Mel. You didn't say he was hot."

I spun around and saw Meredith standing a few feet away by the stairs. Ignoring what she'd said—I'd get her for that later—I released Tyler's hand and took off running. It had been far too long since I'd seen my BFF, I thought as I crashed into her. She smelled like Sunflowers, the perfume by Elizabeth Arden.

"What are you doing here?" I asked, releasing her and taking a step back.

"Your mom said someone needed to pick you up, so I volunteered."

"I didn't know you'd be there today."

Meredith shrugged. "I wanted to see you. Maybe talk fabrics."

I eyed her suspiciously. "If you wanted to meet Tyler, we could have set something up." Her eyes focused on something over my shoulder, and I knew Tyler was near. I leaned back into his chest as he placed his hand on my shoulder. "Meredith, this is Tyler. Tyler, Meredith."

He reached his free hand around me and shook Meredith's hand. "It's nice to meet you. Spice here talks about you a lot."

"Spice?"

"Spice Girls reference," I mumbled, elbowing Tyler in the gut. "Nevermind. Let's go!" I circled my arm around Meredith's, and we skipped towards the parking lot, leaving Tyler behind.

"It's all right. I'll just find my own way."

"He's so cute," Meredith whispered, leaning her head in towards mine.

"I know," I told her. "Stop being dramatic," I yelled back to him. We slowed our pace so he could catch up.

"So, Meredith, will you be my getaway driver if things get crazy?" Tyler asked as we settled in Mer's car.

"Of course."

"Don't encourage him," I interjected.

"We'll just have to come up with some kind of code," she continued as if I hadn't even spoken.

"How about I scratch my nose?"

"Amateur," Meredith said. "What if you actually have an itch on your nose?"

"Hmm, good point. My nose does get itchy quite often."

"You're a dork," I said.

"You love me anyway," he said, and I caught the look Meredith gave me. I gave her a subtle shake of my head. *Just a figure of speech, Mer.*

"How about I drop my napkin?"

Meredith contemplated that for a moment, then agreed. "That works."

"I'm a little insulted you're trying to find ways to escape my family gathering."

"You are not. Keith and I have an escape plan, too. So do you."

"I do not," I feigned shock, but I totally had a plan.

Meredith put her hand over her stomach, and in her most pathetic voice said "Oh, Mom. My cramps hurt so bad. I need to go lay down."

"I don't sound like that," I said, lifting my chin and looking out the passenger window.

"Yeah, actually ya do."

"Whatever. I can't believe you left Keith at the house."

"Oh, he didn't come. He's on call."

"Dr. and Mrs. Rivers. Has a nice ring to it. You getting used to that?"

Meredith radiated joy. "I can't wait. I think we're close to setting a date."

"Congratulations. Mel mentioned she was designing your wedding dress." Tyler said from the back.

"Thanks. I couldn't imagine anyone else making it for me. Melanie is an amazing designer."

"I agree. I wish she'd put herself out there."

"Me too," Meredith said, nudging my elbow with hers.

Tyler asked questions about the area as we drove the short distance to my parents' house. Melanie answered most of them, happy to play tour guide as she drove. *And on your left, the house with all the ornaments in the front yard, known as the eyesore of the community.* We turned onto my parents' street and I felt a familiar wave of comfort roll over me. Right before the nerves set in.

My boyfriend was about to meet my parents.

"We're here!" I said as we pulled up across the street from my parents' home. I looked over my shoulder at Tyler. "You ready for this?"

- 15 -
Tyler

As we got out of the car, I took in the modest brick home in front of me. It was small with dark green shutters and dormer windows that suggested an upper floor. A full maple tree cast shade over one of the windows, and I couldn't help but wonder if Melanie ever used the thick limbs of that tree to sneak out her bedroom window. Was she a rebellious teen or a good girl? I think she leaned towards the latter.

"Come on," she said, grabbing my hand and pulling me across the quiet street. "Everyone is probably around back, but I'd bet anything Mom's in the kitchen."

We walked up three brick steps and through a screen door into the living room. There were two large, worn sofas facing each other with a coffee table in between, and a well-loved recliner in the corner facing a wall-mounted flat screen television. The TV was off, and all the sound was coming from the back of the house.

We followed the delicious aroma of various sweets through the house and stood at the perimeter of the kitchen for a moment before we were noticed. At least a dozen women, who each looked remarkably like Melanie at assorted ages, stood around talking at the same time. There must have been at least three different conversations going, but it seemed all the women were partaking in each one.

The noise level…

I unconsciously took a step back—I think it was survival instinct—and Melanie gave my hand a squeeze.

"Hello, Mom," Melanie called over the ruckus.

Silence. Blessed, lovely silence.

Made awkward by the fact that all the women turned their attention to me.

Melanie tightened her grip on my hand, probably smelling my fear. I hadn't been lying when I told her I never met a girl's parents before. This encounter—an entire extended family—was brand new.

"This is my boyfriend, Tyler." She tugged me into the room and right up to a short thin woman with Melanie's eyes. "Hi, Mama," she said, hugging the small lady. Melanie must have gotten her height from her father.

Her mother looked at her with adoration, in a way I'd guess my mother would have looked at me if she were still alive. When her attention turned to me, her expression was thoughtful.

"It's lovely to finally meet you, Tyler." She spoke perfect English. I'd wrongly assumed she'd have an accent, thanks to that movie. "Melanie has told me so little about you, but I was so pleased to hear she'd be bringing you to our little party today."

"Mom," Melanie whined, making the word several syllables long.

"What? I'm telling the truth."

"You don't always have to be so forthcoming with the info, Ma."

She was blushing again, and I loved it. I thought I was even starting to love her, but aside from my sister and my parents I'd never loved anyone, so I wasn't quite sure what it was supposed to be like. What it was supposed to feel like. I just wanted to be with her all the time. Talk to her. And when I couldn't do either of those things, I thought about her. Was that what it meant to be in love?

Melanie nudged me. "It's a pleasure to meet you, Mrs. Katsaros. I can see where Melanie gets her good looks."

Her mother laughed, not falling for my charm but still mildly entertained. "Aren't you adorable? You can call me Kathy."

"Thank you, Kathy."

"Your father is at the grill. He's been there all afternoon."

"Come on," Melanie said, tugging me along again. "Let's get this out of the way." She stopped by the refrigerator on the way to the back door and pulled out three amber bottles. She handed me two, which I held in my free hand.

"Sam Adams?" I was going to get along great with her dad.

"It's his favorite." She lowered her voice. "It's a peace offering. You're dating his little girl...his only child...you need all the help you can get."

"Thanks for the vote of confidence." I groaned as we exited the house into a screened-in patio, then out to the yard. I spotted Meredith sitting at a table with a few younger women who may have been Mel's cousins. They had the same dark hair and eyes as the older women in the kitchen. Meredith smirked and waved, then said something to the other girls at the table that had them turning to watch me and Melanie approach her dad.

Thanks, Meredith.

"Daddy," Melanie said to the tallest, bulkiest man standing by the grill. Even I had to look up to him, so he was definitely six-five, at a minimum.

"Cupcake!" the big man said, enveloping Melanie into his arms and lifting her off the ground.

"Put me down," she laughed, hitting him on the back. It was clear she was a daddy's girl, and it was also easy to see how much her father adored her.

"Hi, Uncle James, Marty." She nodded to the two other men. I picked out James and his weak beard immediately. "Daddy," she said in that same saccharine sweet voice she'd greeted him with, "this is my boyfriend, Tyler."

Her father visibly stiffened and faced me straight on. *Shit.* He was intimidating.

I held out my hand and hoped my voice didn't crack. "It's nice to meet you, Mr. Katsaros."

He took my hand and shook it. Quite possibly the most firm handshake I'd ever experienced. It also felt like twenty-five silent minutes had passed before he finally let go. "You planning on drinking both of those?" he asked, nodding to the beers in my other hand.

"Oh. No, not at all. This one's for you," I handed him a bottle. "I'll stick with one since I'll be escorting Mel home later."

"You driving?" he asked.

"No, sir. But I like to keep my wits about me when I'm out with your daughter."

Melanie smiled and wrapped herself around my arm again. She made me feel one hundred feet tall, and I needed that in that moment.

Mr. Katsaros nodded. "Listen here, Tyler. I was just telling my brother about the benefits to adding butter to your steaks when you grill them. He doesn't believe me. Melanie said you were some kind of whiz when it came to the grill, so what do you say?"

I let out a whoosh of air. I hadn't even realized I was holding my breath. Steaks. Grilling. Those were things I could talk about.

"Do you mind?" I asked, gesturing to the stainless-steel lid of the impressive grill.

He took a step back, "Go right ahead."

- 16 -
Melanie

"Tyler and your dad seemed to have hit it off." Meredith noted as we watched the two men from across the yard.

"Yeah," I said, pleased but also a little disappointed. I hadn't gotten a second alone with Tyler since I'd introduced him to my dad at the grill and it had been hours. I ducked out to help my mother in the kitchen while he helped my father finish grilling the steaks, then they dominated the conversation as we sat at the table and ate said steaks. Now, who knew what they were talking about, but a few of my male cousins had joined them, as well as my Uncle David.

"What's eating you?" Mer asked. "You jealous?"

"A little." There was no use in lying to Meredith. "I would have liked to introduce him to some other people, but Dad's monopolizing him."

"Admit it, you wanted to show him off to your single cousins."

I scanned the yard for Valerie and Simone. "Yeah, and the worst two already left."

"Oh, don't worry. All the ladies noticed him the moment you guys hit the backyard. That's why I headed out here first. I wanted to see the look on Valerie's face."

Valerie was my cousin, so I loved her, but she

was also a class A bitch. She always had a new guy on her arm and always flaunted him at family events. She was the first one with a snide remark about my singledom. Her father, my Uncle Gus, was probably rolling in his grave at the parade of men she flounced around with. Also, the fact that he was in his grave was the only reason Valerie got away with half the shit she pulled. There were no other male uncles on my mother's side to take over the paternal role, and my Aunt Maria — Valerie's mother — was still a grieving widow, so she didn't know what to do with her. Or she didn't care. Either way.

"What did Val say?"

"Not much. She just gaped when you walked outside hand-in-hand, then muttered something to Simone, but she must not have liked whatever Simone had to say because she flaked off shortly after that. Didn't even last until dinner." Simone was Valerie's older, non-bitchy sister.

"Oh well. Her loss."

"Damn straight. Those steaks were delicious."

I rolled my eyes. If I didn't hear about steaks again for a month, it would be too soon.

"Hey Spice," Tyler said in my ear as he wrapped his arms around my middle from behind. "What are you two ladies talking about?"

"Not much. Just how you and my dad are BFFs."

"He's a really cool guy," Tyler said, resting his chin on my shoulder. "I can't believe we never talked about him being a cop."

"Would it have made you any less nervous to meet him?"

"Hell no," he laughed. "Good call."

"I'm glad you two got along today. That's important to me."

"What's important to you is important to me," he said, then kissed my cheek.

"It is getting late, though, we'll probably need to catch a train out soon."

"No problem, Spice. Let's say goodbye."

This time Tyler took *my* hand and led me to each of the remaining party guests to say goodbye.

Just before he kissed me goodnight in front of my apartment door, he asked "Did I tell you today how beautiful you are?" I shook my head. "Well, you are. You look beautiful today, and every day for that matter. Just in case I ever forget to tell you again."

He was just too good to be true.

***

"You have *so* much stamina," I practically panted as Tyler rolled off me, taking the sheet with him. "Give that back," I said, yanking it over my naked body.

He rolled so he was facing me and tugged me into him. "You know I'll keep you warm."

I smiled and looked him over, taking in his skin, dewy with sweat. He was so good looking, and he was *mine*.

I nestled my head into his chest and let my mind wander to the week ahead. I had tons of things to do in the office with Fashion Week coming up. Brianna was giving me more responsibilities this year, including attending some events with her, and I couldn't wait. I lived for

Fashion Week. I loved seeing what all the designers had prepared for their shows. I'd never attended before, only stalked everything online, so this was going to be a surreal experience for sure. I wondered if *You're the Man* had any representation at the event, they had a couple pages of fashion.

"Will you be at Fashion Week with Roger?"

Tyler groaned and rolled away from me. "Don't say his name."

"Sorry. Will you be at Fashion Week with your boss?"

"Not even referrals."

I laughed. "I'll be there with Brianna," I told him.

"I have no plans to be there. Hanging around with a bunch of pretentious-"

"A bunch of pretentious what?" I asked, sitting up. I held the sheet tightly against my chest and stared down at him. If that's what he thought about people in the fashion industry…

He closed his eyes and slowly shook his head. "Shit. I didn't mean you."

"Uh huh." I started reaching around for my discarded clothing. Sock, pants, bra, other sock…where the hell was my shirt?

Tyler grabbed my arm, halting my search. "I'm sorry, Mel. I wasn't thinking. I've been to a few fashion things with Roger, and it's his people…they're all…I don't even know what to call them. I didn't mean to group you with them. I'm sorry."

"You know this is my thing, right? This is what I want to do with the rest of my life?"

He shifted to face me and ran his hands up and down my arms. "I know it is, and I love seeing the sparkle in your eyes when you talk about it. The industry just hasn't been as kind to me as it has been to you."

"That's because you've only been exposed to one small part," I started, defending the fashion industry that I firmly believed was part of the fabric of my being. Pun intended.

"Babe, I know. Are we gonna argue about this?"

I sighed. I did *not* want to argue with Tyler. Unless we were arguing about the merits of our decades of choice, it just wasn't fun.

"No, we're not going to argue about this," I finally said. "But it is going to take up a lot of my time for the next couple weeks. Brianna is entertaining a lot of designers to try to get an edge."

"We'll work it out," he said, offering me a small smile. He laid back down and pulled me against his side.

I rested my head on his bare chest and listened to the sound of his heartbeat. He said we'd work it out, but something about how he said it felt...off. I stared at the wall, stuck in my own head, until the rhythmic rise and fall of his chest helped me drift me off to sleep.

- 17 -
Tyler

"What's Melanie up to?" Hannah asked over the low din of the restaurant. "I assumed she'd come with us."

My sister stopped by my desk after a morning visit with Preston and asked me to lunch. Under normal circumstances, the big boss's wife coming to see me at work would have sent me into a tailspin—sister or not—but seeing as though Roger was out of the office, a fact Hannah had apparently confirmed before coming down, I didn't much care.

"Fashion Week stuff."

"You don't sound too happy about that." She eyed me over her steaming mug of hot tea, perceptive as ever that sister of mine.

"Why are you drinking hot tea at lunch?" I wondered, attempting to change the subject.

"Because I like it. Don't change the subject. What's going on?"

I sighed. "Nothing is going on. She's just busy helping her boss get ready for Fashion Week."

"And again, I say...you don't sound happy about that."

"How do you want me to sound? I work in the fashion industry," I droned on. "It hasn't been kind to me." I said, knowing I was echoing my conversation with Melanie, but Hannah didn't know that. "I'm sorry I can't show the proper level of enthusiasm."

"You're being such a baby," Hannah said, shaking her head.

"Excuse me?"

"Just because you're not happy with your job doesn't mean you can't be happy for Melanie."

That wasn't what I was doing.

Was that what I was doing?

And how did Hannah know I wasn't happy with my job?

Hannah continued. "And before you deny it, I know you hate working for the magazine. Or for Roger. Whatever. It's written all over your face any time I ask you about work and you immediately change the subject. I catch glimpses of you at your desk from the elevator sometimes, too. Jesus, Ty. You look miserable. If you hate it so much, why don't you quit? You won't hurt Preston's feelings. Maybe he can even-"

"Stop right there." Hannah knew I wouldn't take handouts from family. I'd already burdened them enough over the years, even though they'd never admit it.

She sighed. "I'm just worried about you."

"Don't be worried about me."

"I'm your sister, it's in the handbook. You've got a great thing with Mel, and I don't want you to mess it up."

"Thanks for the vote of confidence."

"Tyler...I've known you a long time." I rolled my eyes. "I've seen you end relationships over petty things. I'd hate to see what happens when you're faced with a real challenge."

She wasn't entirely wrong, but that wasn't the

case with me and Mel. We were good. Solid, even. Sure, Mel was spending more time with her boss than me these days, but I understood. *She* actually loved her job. No one was messing anything up, especially not me.

"Is that how you're getting your exercise these days, sis?" She looked at me funny. "By jumping to conclusions?" It was her turn to roll her eyes. "There's no issue with me and Mel. We're good. No one is ending anything. And I am happy for her," I continued. "She's exactly where she wants to be, and I admire that about her."

"Well, not *exactly* where she wants to be, I'd bet. I think she'd rather be one of the ones in the show, instead of behind the scenes."

"Yeah, you're right. She's an amazing designer. Do you know she designs almost every outfit she wears? One day she'll make it, I know she will, and she'll have made all those contacts working for Brianna and already have two feet in the door of the industry."

"What's she waiting for?"

"I don't know. Her best friend has been trying to get her to show her boss her designs, but I think she's afraid."

"She shouldn't be. They really are amazing."

I shrugged my shoulders. "I've told her the same thing."

"You should motivate her, Ty. That's one of the many jobs of a significant other. We're that ever-present driving force behind our spouses, driving them to be successful."

"So you're the reason Preston is a millionaire?"

"One of the many," she winked. "But seriously, you should encourage her to share her designs with someone. She's been working for Brianna for a while, surely she has already made the acquaintance of *someone* she can share them with. Preston said Brianna spoke highly of her, I'd bet if she shared them with Brianna, she would take care of her."

"Maybe."

"I wish you'd let Preston help you."

"Han-"

"I know, I know. You don't want any help. But I can tell you're not happy and it's in my nature to fix that. I can't help it."

"You're a good sister."

"I'm your *best* sister."

"You're my only sister."

She balled up her napkin and threw it at me. Despite the Town Car and driver waiting outside the restaurant, the powder blue Chanel suit with the Louboutin shoes, and all the matching Tiffany jewelry, my sister was still my sister. She was still that awkward tomboy I grew up with.

And she still couldn't throw to save her life; the napkin missed my face by a foot. Hannah blushed and muttered a quiet apology to the woman at the table beside us whose shoulder it bounced off.

"Quit messing around," I playfully scolded, laughing and pointing a stern finger at her.

"You look just like Dad when you do that."

I stopped laughing, took a sip of my drink.

"Sorry, Ty."

"Don't be." I looked like my father. Nothing to be ashamed of.

"I know-"

"It's fine, Han." I looked at my watch. "I have to get back to work."

"No, you don't. Roger isn't even there."

"I still have work to do," I told her, taking cash out of my wallet for a tip.

"I know the owner," she joked.

I stood and walked to her side of the table, giving her a kiss on the head. "I'll see you for dinner this weekend."

"Bring Melanie. She's your meal ticket," Hannah warned with a smile.

"I will." I left the restaurant and nodded to Hannah's driver as I passed by. It was a short walk back to the office, and I needed to feel the crisp, cold air.

I hoped I would be bringing Melanie to dinner on Sunday, but I'd talked to her for all of thirty minutes this week and it was already Thursday. The few texts I sent went unanswered for hours. Two of the three phone calls we had were so late, she'd fallen asleep on the phone. I may have stayed on the line and listened to her soft breathing for a few seconds before hanging up. Creepy as that may be, the truth was I missed her. I missed her a lot. She'd become such a large part of my life in such a short period of time. She was having such a great time, too, doing what she was doing. It stung because she was having that fun without me, and she didn't seem to mind.

Hannah was right. I *was* being a baby.

I pulled out my phone and fired off a quick text, surprised when she replied right away.

Tyler: I hope you are having a good day.
Melanie: I'm having the best day.
Tyler: That's great, Spice. Tell me about it over dinner this weekend?

Melanie: I wish I could, but Brianna has us booked all through next week. Raincheck?
Tyler: Sure.

- 18 -
Melanie

Fashion Week was as amazing as I'd dreamed it would be.

In my four years working for Brianna, this was the first time she requested that I be by her side through it all, and I was so grateful. The lights and the glamour were everything I thought they would be. I reveled in being in the middle of it all, and then I went home and stayed awake imagining running one of the shows myself. Dressing the statuesque models in my designs and sending them down the runway. The flashing lights of the photographers' cameras capturing images of *my* clothing line and splashing them all over the pages of magazines like *Leading Lady* and *Vogue*.

But through it all...I missed Tyler. I missed him so much. I hadn't had an actual free minute during the day to call or see him in nearly two weeks, and I felt guilty calling him before I started my day or when I got home, knowing it was ridiculously early or way too late. I'd already fallen asleep on the phone with him too many times.

Fashion Week was almost over though, and while I was having the time of my life, I was also relieved that my life would finally be returning to normal. No more eighteen-hour days on my feet in crazy heels. I wasn't sure how the elite walked in these shoes all day long. I actually lost feeling in two of my toes and expected them to fall off any day now. My personal closet consisted of more practical selections, but because I was on Brianna's arm, I had access to the sample closet and was expected to dress accordingly, mainly as a nod to the designers we were visiting at the show, but also in an effort to blend in with the rest of the beautiful people.

By day, we were at shows and by night, we were mingling at whatever restaurant or club was hosting the best party, sometimes more than one a night. It was exhausting, but the food and drinks were delicious, and the company was decent. Tonight's locale was *The Theater*. It was dark with a vintage theater theme. Candlelight sconces dotted the walls between dark, velvet curtains. Ornate chandeliers hung from the ceiling, and what looked like actual candles burned in them. The theme made no sense to me because we were in Tribeca, nowhere near the theater district, but whatever. Maybe it had to do with the annual film festival. There were always going to be some things I didn't understand about this world.

"I'm so impressed with your work this week, Melanie," Brianna said, turning my attention from the decor. "You've been such an asset to me this week. I can't thank you enough." She tapped her wine glass against mine in cheers.

"Thank you for the opportunity to be here. I've dreamed of what Fashion Week was like my whole life. This is pretty amazing." I blushed, partially from the alcohol and partially from my rookie confession.

Brianna leaned in and confided, "I used to

dream of this, too."

I returned her smile and relaxed. I truly had the best boss. Maybe Meredith was right. Maybe I could share my designs with Brianna. She had told me my outfits were cute once or twice, maybe she would support me in my ultimate goal of being a designer.

Gathering some courage, I leaned forward to confess the underlying reason I applied to work for the magazine four years ago, but Brianna spoke first.

"There's something I'd like to ask you, or rather, offer you. Another opportunity."

"I'm listening," I said, intrigued. *Was Brianna a mind reader?* I doubted that.

"I'll be gone the next two weeks...London and Milan," she said, not that she needed to remind me where the next two fashion weeks would take place. "I'll finish the month in Paris and have some additional work to do there as we're considering establishing a French sister magazine, *Femme De Tête*. I could really use the assistance of my assistant," she giggled, the wine loosening her up as I'd witnessed a few other evenings this week.

I softly laughed with her, until I realized what she was asking. She was asking *me* to go to Paris Fashion Week with *her*.

"You're an amazing assistant, Melanie. You always have been. You're a little quiet in the office, so before I asked you to go to Paris with me, I needed to make sure you could handle yourself in that kind of environment, which is why I had you accompany me the past two weeks. You go above and beyond outside of the office, just as you do inside the office. Like I said earlier, you've impressed me. It's not often that staff impress me, to be honest. I set extremely high expectations, and you're constantly surpassing them. I appreciate that."

"Wow. Brianna, I don't even know what to say." I was speechless. This was probably the most I'd heard Brianna say to one person in four years and the fact that it was all praise directed at me had me gobsmacked.

"Say you'll come!" She smiled, taking another sip of her chardonnay.

"Of course. I would be honored."

"Yay," she said, clapping her hands together like a schoolgirl, nearly spilling her wine. Maybe I'd underestimated how many she'd had to drink.

I tried to match her enthusiasm, but then I realized...I'd have to tell Tyler I'd be going to Paris. Another week spent away from him, and this time an ocean apart. If it was difficult to keep in touch while in the same city, I couldn't imagine what it would be like when we were in different time zones.

- 19 –
Tyler

"I missed you so much," I said, my lips and tongue making their way up Melanie's body. Fashion Week ended last night and after she slept in a little this morning, Melanie came straight to my apartment. That was ten hours ago, and it was starting to get dark. "I missed you, too," she said around a groan.

I rolled off her and she frowned. "Hey now…" she said.

"What?" I asked. "We've been at it since ten o'clock this morning. I'm tired and famished."

"You're such a tease," she whined.

"First, I do believe you're fully satisfied. Second, I'll show you a tease," I said, and she smirked. "After I eat."

She frowned again and slapped my bare ass.

"Ouch," I said, rubbing it as I climbed out of bed. "Just for that, I'm not letting you pick the grub." I pulled on a pair of sweatpants and walked the short distance to my folder of takeout menus, stepping around our discarded clothing as I went.

"Can we just get pizza? I swear those fashion people only eat salads. I need some pizza in my life."

"Pizza, it is." I knew I said she wasn't picking the food, but no self-respecting New Yorker turned down pizza. Using the delivery app, I placed my order and returned to bed, sitting up against the headboard. She cuddled against me, her head in my lap, and I stroked my hand down her back.

It sucked being without her...missing her...being with her again felt right.

"I have some news," Melanie said, and I looked down at her dark, messy hair. She wasn't looking at me. I internally sighed, hoping this wasn't bad news.

"What's up?" I asked, attempting to sound nonchalant. I don't think it worked because I felt her stiffen against me ever so slightly.

"Brianna invited me to go to Paris at the end of the month."

And there it was...the other shoe that always dropped. Was this how it would always be? This was the industry that Melanie wanted to be in. It would involve shit like this on the regular, right? Flying off to Paris, London, and Milan for the Fashion Weeks twice a year. Who knew where else she'd end up needing to go? L.A.? Everyone who was anyone ended up having to go to L.A. for something, and if I knew anything, it was that Melanie would end up being someone.

"You're not saying anything," she said, now peeking up at me through her hair.

I gave her my best fake smile. "It's probably a great opportunity for you, right?"

"Yeah. Brianna told me I was an amazing assistant, and she was really impressed with my work."

"That's great, Spice." I said, my tone sounding dull even to my own ears.

"Is it though? Because you seem...I don't

know."

I thought about what to say, then I thought about my conversation with Hannah. I should be happy for Melanie because she's on her way to making her dreams come true. I should be focused on her, because that's what significant others do...they support the people they loved.

Wait, did I love Melanie?

I thought so. At least, it sure felt like I did. I couldn't stop thinking about her. I wanted to be with her all the time, or at least talk to her. She was an amazing woman and she had a cool family. I was happy with her. I think maybe I did love her.

And suddenly...I wanted to tell her just that.

I smiled down at her, looking deep into her dark green eyes. "I'm fine, baby. I just love you."

Her eyes widened, then filled with tears as she smiled up at me. "I love you, too."

I moved down the bed to kiss her, and the moment our lips connected, nothing had ever felt so right.

***

"Mmm," Melanie hummed as she devoured her fourth slice of plain cheese pizza. I was glad I'd ordered two pies; my girl had an appetite. "This is sooo good."

"I'll tell you what else is *sooo* good," I said, wiggling my eyebrows.

Melanie shook her head. "Nope, a fresh and hot cheese pizza is better than sex, too."

I raised an eyebrow, gaping at her in disbelief. I loved pizza...but I wasn't sure anything was better than sex. She looked so damn content though, shoveling the mixture of dough, sauce, and cheese in her mouth. I'd let this one go; the girl obviously needed her pizza.

"How has it been at work since he-who-shall-not-be-named hasn't been there?"

"Quiet. Think you're going to tell Brianna about your designs since you two have been spending so much time together?"

"I don't know. I almost did, but before I could get the words out, she asked me to go to Paris."

"Really?" I was so proud of her for trying.

"Yeah. I just don't want her to be disappointed that I don't want to be her assistant forever though, you know?"

I laughed. "I don't think she expects you to be her assistant forever. You said it yourself, she's impressed with your work. She probably knows you have bigger and better things in your future than just being her assistant."

"I could say the same thing about you," she said.

"Yeah, well, the difference between me and you is that your boss recognizes your work."

"He may not admit it, but your boss recognizes your work, too. He has to since you're the one doing his job. You could run that magazine-"

"I don't want to run the magazine."

"I know you don't, but you could."

"What's with all the women in my life getting on me about my job? First Hannah, then you." I was starting to get pissed off.

"Because you hate it?"

"Yeah, so let's not talk about it."

"I just think you can do so much more, and you're settling for whatever reason."

"How is what I'm doing any different from what you're doing? I want to write, so I'm working my way into the industry. Same as you."

"But you're not writing, Ty. I'm still designing—doing what I love—while I work for Brianna. You're just working for Roger. You're not doing what you love."

"I grill. I enjoy grilling."

"Then write about it. Start a blog or something. That could help get you in the industry as well. I can't tell you how many fashion bloggers Brianna hires on a freelance basis for the magazine."

The idea had merit...but I didn't know anything about starting a blog. Did guys even blog? Hell, I probably had some kind of non-compete clause in my contract anyway. It was no use.

I blew out a breath, then groaned. Adulting was difficult. "I don't know."

"Then write something and give it to Roger. *You're the Man* would really benefit from some lifestyle features like food and exercise." It wasn't the first time she'd suggested that.

"I agree with you, but if you think Roger would accept a recommendation from me, or better yet, an article, you're nuts."

Melanie's shoulders slumped in defeat, and I felt bad, but it didn't change the facts. Roger would never go for anything I suggested.

- 20 -
Melanie

"I can't believe you're going to Paris," Meredith's voice crackled across the line.

I stuffed a few pairs of pajamas in my suitcase and smiled. "I know, it's like a dream come true."

"It's like you're getting to sample everything you'll experience when you're a big-time fashion designer!"

"It's crazy, Mer, because not all the designers at these shows are big time. Brianna has an eye for the underdogs. There are a lot of designers who are fresh out the gate at these shows. It's really neat to see." I pulled a couple pairs of leggings, three tunics, and a sweater out of my closet and set them on the bed to fold. The magazine was shipping clothes from the sample closet to Paris for me, so I could pack light, which was great because that meant I'd have plenty of room in my luggage to take all my Paris purchases home.

"Even more reason for you to share your stuff with her. If she appreciates new designers *and* she appreciates you, then voila. You're golden, lady." Couldn't say I hadn't thought of that myself.

"I know. I'm just not ready yet. It's too crazy a time right now and my news would just get lost in the chaos of Fashion Week. I think I'll say something when we get back."

"Good plan. You'd just better do it."

"I will, I promise."

"So, how's Prince Charming?"

"Ugh," I groan, adding some socks and underwear to my suitcase. "Why are you calling him that?"

"Because he is sweep-you-off-your-feet amazing, that's why."

"That's true, but he'd be appalled if you called him that."

"Where is he anyway? You leave tomorrow, I figured you two would be hanging out."

"We had lunch today, but he's out with a friend tonight."

"Wait. He's out with a friend instead of being with you the night before you leave to go out of the country for a week?"

"Glad you've been paying attention." I flopped down on my bed, messing up my neat pile of folded clothes. "He's been a bit off the last couple weeks."

"Off how?"

"I don't know," I said, watching my relationship with Tyler like a highlight reel in my mind. The good parts made me smile to myself. "He told me he loved me."

"What?!" I winced at my best friend's shriek. "And you didn't call me immediately?" I could have thrown it in her face that she waited to tell me she'd gotten engaged, but I refrained.

"Sorry. It's just been crazy over here with Brianna being out of town, recovering from Fashion Week, and getting ready for Paris."

"Well, what about him telling you he loves you makes it seem like he's off?"

I look around my small apartment. "Because

he's not here? Because he was so nonchalant about the fact that I'm going out of the country for a week?"

"I'm sorry, sweetie. Maybe he's just going to miss you so he's sad about it and distancing himself. Guys aren't always in touch with their emotions the way we are."

"Tell me something I don't know."

"I know, that's not new news, I just wanted to remind you because we don't always think rationally when we're upset. He might just be being a guy, you know? No harm meant."

"Yeah...I guess."

"Don't let it get you down. You're going to Paris! And the week will be over before you know it, and you'll be back home in his arms."

I smiled, picturing us lying in his bed together this morning. I couldn't wait to be back in that very same place in a week. "You're right."

"Okay, girl. I've got to go. We're having dinner with Keith's parents tonight to talk about the rehearsal dinner. We don't even have a date set yet, but his mom wants to plan."

I laughed. "She's excited. Her only son is getting married, and she doesn't have a daughter. Give her some credit."

"I hate it when you're right. Have a great time in Paris. Take lots of pictures."

"I will. Love you, bye."

"Bye."

The call disconnected, and I stared at my silent phone on the bed. Closing my eyes, I brought back up the image of Tyler and me in bed this morning. What I wouldn't give to be back in that bed with him. My gaze shifted to my key ring, hanging from the hook by the door. Every time my parents visited me in the city, my father reminded me how stupid it was to keep my key ring right by the door. I never moved it. My key ring held the key to my apartment, and if they were already in the apartment, what difference would it make where my key ring was? But...my key ring didn't only hold my key anymore. It held Tyler's key, too. He'd given it to me one day when he had an event after work and needed a clean shirt. I had time, and he didn't, so I went and got it for him. He never asked for the key back, and I had forgotten all about it.

Almost.

Maybe I'd surprise him tonight...be waiting for him in bed when he got back from his night out with the guys. Would that be crazy of me? Or would he love it?

I didn't give it another thought. I slipped on my flats, pulled a sweater on over my tank top, and grabbed my bag and keys. I gave one last look at my unfinished packing and vowed to get back home early enough in the morning to finish before the car came to pick me up at nine.

- 21 -
Melanie

The cab ride was quick. The ease in hailing the cab and the lack of traffic made me feel like I was doing the right thing. The universe was making it too easy for me to get to his place for it to have been a bad idea.

I smiled at the doorman. I couldn't remember his name, but I'd seen him a few times before. I took the elevator to the tenth floor and got out, nervously making my way down the hall to his apartment. I wasn't sure why I was nervous. He wasn't home. I shook off the nerves and stopped in front of his door.

I took a deep breath and slowly stuck the key in the lock and turned. As I heard the click of the lock disengaging, I heard some rustling from the common area. Panicking at the thought of getting caught—though I wasn't entirely sure why—I quickly opened the door, slipped inside, and slammed it shut. I leaned my back against the door and closed my eyes, my breath coming like I'd just run up the ten flights.

Then it registered...the television was on. Well, not a television because Tyler didn't have one, but his laptop. Some cop TV show was playing.

I opened one eye and took in a slice of the brightly lit apartment before me. A bit too lit up considering Tyler wasn't home. Then I opened the other eye and let them both wander around the room.

I froze when I met Tyler's eyes.

He was sitting up in his bed, decked out in blue plaid pajama pants and a white t-shirt. He had a handful of popcorn halfway to his mouth.

"Hi," I said, stunned.

"Hi," he said, also stunned.

"What are you doing here?" I asked, my back still stuck to his door.

"I live here?" He said it like it was a question. I didn't blame him. I'd just barrel-assed through his front door like a psychopath, and *I* was asking *him* what he was doing in his own apartment.

"Of course. I thought you were out," I said, taking one step away from the door.

He sighed and dropped the popcorn into the bowl. "I'm sorry…I lied."

Tears pricked the back of my eyes, but I didn't let them fall. Why was I even going to cry? Because he lied to me? Why would he lie to me? Why would he say he was going out but stay home? Did he not want to see me? That was it…wasn't it…he didn't want to see me.

"Oh," I said as realization dawned. "I'm just gonna go then."

"No, Mel, wait." He was up and in front of me in a flash. "It's nothing bad, I swear."

"I asked you to be with me tonight, and you lied to get out of it. What isn't bad about that?" I wasn't upset anymore, now I was just mad. Now he was going to lie about lying?

Tyler groaned. "It's not like that. I mean it is, but it isn't. I'm gonna miss you, Mel. I didn't want to say goodbye to you tonight, okay? I knew if we hung out, I'd just be waiting until the end of the night when you had to say goodbye, and I fucking hate saying goodbye. It was a stupid way of going about it, but I didn't think you'd find out."

"And that makes it okay?" I asked, feeling a little less mad at him.

"No. It doesn't make it okay." Tyler covered his face with his hands and sighed. "I'm bad at this, Melanie." He looked me in the eyes. "I've never been in a serious relationship before. I've had other relationships, but they were never like me and you. I never really cared what they were doing, and I don't think they cared what I was doing either. When things got too real, I did something stupid to screw it up. I don't want to do that with you, and I'm so afraid that one day I will, like I almost did tonight. Please don't tell me I screwed this up for good?"

As much of an adult as Tyler was, I could see that part of him was still that young boy whose parents left and never came home.

I lifted my hand to his cheek and felt the light stubble there. "You didn't screw this up for good."

Tyler let out a big breath. "Thank you," he said, kissing my forehead and pulling me into his chest.

I pulled away, and he frowned. "You have to talk to me, Ty. I'm not a relationship expert either, but I know that people who are in relationships have to communicate with each other. It's the only way it's going to work. We talk pretty well with each other, don't you think?"

He nodded. "Yeah, I do."

"Then just talk to me next time you're feeling this way, okay? I don't want to say goodbye to you either. I'm going to miss you so much. I feel like we have barely seen each other this month because my job has had me so busy, but I still love you."

"I love you, too," he said, giving me a quick kiss.

I smiled and let him hold me again. It felt so right being in his arms, but part of me was still upset that he'd lied instead of just talking to me about it.

"But I have to ask…what *are* you doing here? And why did you come flying in the door like you were being chased?"

I groaned into his chest. "I heard someone in the hall. Don't even ask. I'd be a terrible spy. We'll leave it at that. And I just wanted to see you. I was remembering being in bed with you this morning and I missed that. I wanted to be here waiting for you when you got home tonight."

"You're the sweetest person I've ever met," he said, holding me tighter.

"So I've been told…"

He laughed. "Come on…I'm watching old episodes of *CSI*."

I kicked off my shoes as he pulled me over to his bed. We laid down in our usual position, with him propped up by pillows and me alongside him with my head resting on his chest. He pressed play on the computer screen, and we watched the Vegas forensics team do their thing.

I fell asleep in my favorite place, listening to his heartbeat.

Morning came way too soon.

- 22 -
Tyler

So you see, folks...whether you are using an elaborate stainless steel machine in your backyard, a small charcoal grill on your balcony, or a countertop appliance in your galley-style kitchen, the possibilities are endless.

I watched the cursor blink rapidly at the end of the last paragraph.

I'd finally done it.

I drafted a city grilling article. I'd need to practice some different recipes using different grills and techniques before I could write the next column, but I completed the introduction to the series and after re-reading it for a third time, I thought it was pretty damn good.

Whether or not anyone else would ever read it was yet to be determined. Melanie had a ridiculous amount of faith in me, but she also had a great boss who would probably support her desire to be more than just an executive assistant. My boss probably wasn't even aware of what my official job title was. Peon Gopher Boy was not it.

I jotted down a few spices to grab from the corner store and some meat I needed from the butcher, then sent a text to Hannah telling her I'd be utilizing their massive grill that evening. She never cared, but I always wanted to announce myself, not wanting to drop by uninvited. She and Preston acted like an old married couple, but I was sure they still did things I didn't want to walk in on. As expected, she replied for me to come over any time, so I grabbed my wallet and keys, and left the apartment.

***

"What is that flavor?" Hannah asked around a moan as she chewed another piece of filet.

"Try this piece," I said, ignoring her previous question. I couldn't share all my secrets, even with my sister. She glared at me but took the offered fork and put the meat in her mouth.

"Mmm, this is good, too. But it tastes the same."

I grinned. Just what I'd been hoping for. "One was grilled on your electric grill in the kitchen, the other on the grill out back."

"No way," she said.

"Yes way."

"How do you do that?"

"A magician never tells." I said, setting the plates down on the table in front of her.

Hannah rolled her eyes. "Whatever. If you won't tell me, you'll just have to keep coming over here and making me steaks."

"As long as you're buying." The two small filets I picked up at the butcher on the way over cost twenty bucks a pop. I couldn't afford to make that a habit.

"I would gladly stock my fridge with filet mignon and any other kind of meat if you came over and grilled for me on the regular." She pulled over the plate with the counter-cooked filet and cut off another piece. "It's uncanny how you are able to capture the taste of the grill in something that was cooked in the kitchen."

I shrugged. "Practice makes perfect." Also, the right seasoning blend did wonders.

"How's Melanie?"

I smiled, thinking of my girl. "She's great."

"Is she enjoying Paris?"

"I think so. Brianna's kept her pretty busy, so she's exhausted, but the whole thing is right up her alley, so I think she's enjoying it."

"It's like an immersion experience...she's been dropped right in the center of the fashion universe. Must be nerve-wracking."

"Yeah, sounds about right...she eats that shit up, though. She's fearless. She dives into every opportunity headfirst." A quality I really, really wish I possessed. Maybe if I had even half the courage she had, I'd be doing something different with my life.

Hannah smiled a dreamy smile at me. "You really do love her."

Now it was my turn to roll my eyes.

"Seriously, though," she said, taking a sip of her wine.

It was a Cabernet Sauvignon I chose from their cellar to pair with the filets. That was another feature I thought to add to the grilling column, wine pairings for those who wanted to add an upscale aspect to their grilling.

"I see the look in your eyes when you think about her. You get all cloudy and dreamy. You're totally in love with her."

"What's your point?" I asked, trying not to bark

at my sister but losing my patience. I knew I loved Melanie. I didn't need Hannah droning on and on about it.

"It's just nice to see you happy, little brother. That's all." She took another sip of wine and started to get up from her chair. I went and scared her out of her own kitchen with my grizzliness.

"It's nice to be happy," I offered. "In a relationship, that is." Hannah paused and sat back down, seeming to sense I wasn't finished.

I wasn't sure what else I wanted to say, but I thought back to the conversation we'd had over lunch in Central Park months ago. I'd 'fessed up to Melanie about self-sabotaging my previous relationships, but I hadn't admitted it to Hannah. I didn't know why it was easier to admit that to Melanie, but not to my sister.

I let out a deep sigh. "You were right...I did sabotage my previous relationships. I left them — or got them to leave me — before they decided to leave me. Before you say anything, I know it's a Mommy and Daddy issue of mine, and I'm working on it. I don't know why Melanie is different, but she just is."

"Does she know about all this?"

"Yes. We've talked about my dating history and my...issues."

Hannah's eyes widened. "Really?"

"Yes, Han. This is the real deal with Melanie. I don't want to screw it up. I told her as much."

"That's really great, Ty." She got up from the table and wrapped her thin arms around me and squeezed. She smelled of something floral, just like our Mom used to. I always wondered if the connection was just in my head, or if Hannah had taken to Mom's perfume, but I never asked. I figured if Hannah was using the same perfume as Mom, it was her personal choice to do so and none of my business. It was a familiar and comfortable scent, though, so I liked it.

"Thanks for letting me do all this over here tonight," I said, squeezing her back.

"No problem. Gonna tell me what you're up to?"

"Not yet."

"Okay," she said, pulling away. "You're welcome here any time, as long as you feed me and clean up after yourself."

"Deal," I agreed, then I got to work clearing the table.

- 23 -
Melanie

"Oh, Ty," I moaned, licking my lips. "This is amazing."

"We haven't even gotten to the best part," he said, sliding another plate across the marble counter.

We were sitting at the counter in his sister's kitchen. She and Preston were out for the night and had given Tyler permission to wine and dine me at their house. Apparently, Tyler had been a busy boy while I was away, testing — and mastering — a bunch of different recipes on the grill.

"What's this?" I asked, rubbing my hands together in preparation.

"These are grilled bananas smothered in chocolate sauce and covered with crushed, grilled almonds."

"Oh. My. God. You grilled dessert?" I asked, wowed.

My dad had grilled all the time when I was growing up, but he never made dessert. Or pizza, for that matter, which Ty had offered up tonight as an appetizer. Grilled pizza?! Could you believe it? It was ah-mazing.

Tyler offered a wicked grin. "Just wait until you taste it, Spice."

I shivered from the desire in his eyes. I'd gotten

home from Paris late yesterday evening and promptly crashed, then I had to take care of some things at the office today, so Tyler and I didn't see each other until lunch. He brought me my favorite gazpacho soup from the Spanish deli down the street, and I ate it at my desk while I busily returned emails and sent personal notes to some of the connections I'd made in Paris. After work, I was exhausted. He called us a car to take us to Hannah's so we could enjoy dinner together and some alone time.

Dinner had been amazing. It was one grilled course after another. We had a grilled vegetable salad, grilled caprese pizza with tomatoes, basil, and mozzarella cheese, and then he perfectly prepared two swordfish fillets and grilled some tiny potatoes and more veggies for sides. Everything was delicious, and he even prepared some of it on an indoor grill. He was so talented, and I hoped that one day he would be able to put that talent to good use.

"Mmm," I moaned some more as I tasted the chocolate covered bananas. The chocolate sauce had a hint of amaretto that was set off by the crushed almonds. "You are a grill god."

He laughed. "That's a new one."

"It won't be the last time you hear it, I promise." He winked, then cleared some of the extra plates out of the way as I continued to stuff my face with the chocolate deliciousness. "Are you trying some new recipes or something?" I wondered.

He rinsed off a plate before sticking it in the dishwasher, then turned off the sink and looked at me. "I started writing some draft columns."

My grin went from ear to ear. "Really? That's fantastic!" I jumped off my stool and ran around the counter to hug him. I was so happy he was finally doing it. "What are you writing about? How do you feel? Can I read them?"

Tyler laughed and kissed the top of my head. "Calm down, Spice. I've only written a couple pieces so far. I'm just trying some different things out to see if I can find my groove, so-to-speak. I'd love for you to read them, just not yet. I want to do at least one more read through of each one first."

"I'm so proud of you," I whispered, my head still against his chest. "I love that you're doing this...that you're going after what you want. It's so cool, Ty."

"Thanks, baby."

***

"Paris at night was so beautiful. The little shops and cafes and the streetlights and old architecture. It's so hard to describe." I snuggled deeper into his side, my head laying on his bare chest. We were back at my apartment, in my bed. He'd wake early in the morning to go back to his place to change before work. I'd have him leave things here, but there truly was no room. Same with his place. We may need to rectify that one day.

"Well, I guess I'm just going to have to go with you when you show your designs during fashion week and see what there is to see in Paris."

I loved that he said it so matter-of-factly, like there wasn't a doubt in his mind that I would be showing my designs in fashion week one day. He believed in me so thoroughly, just as I believed in him. I was so happy he was starting to explore his writing. There was definitely something there and once he found it, he was going to thrive.

"Did you meet any cool people?" he asked.

"Tons! I met so many designers and a lot of them were very down to earth. I was afraid they'd be pretentious or too overwhelmed to talk, but they were really great. One designer was brand new and so nervous, but her designs were beautiful. She used such vibrant colors, and the outfits were things normal people would wear. It gave me hope, you know?"

"Yeah, that's great. I'm glad you got to see that."

"Me too. I was kind of afraid, you know? I mean I've worked in the field long enough to know that there are tons of different designs because there are a lot of different tastes to appeal to, but I'd always hoped I'd land myself with a runway show like what's at the fashion weeks, but I wasn't sure if my *normal* stuff would make it there. But this gave me hope."

"You're gonna do big things Melanie Athena Katsaros. Big things." He kissed my forehead again, and I closed my eyes.

"You'll do big things, too, Tyler Scott." I sat up, holding the sheet to my chest. "Wait a second. How do I not know your middle name?"

Tyler laughed. "Because I never told you." He pulled me back down beside him and tucked me into the Melanie-sized nook by his side.

"Why not?" I asked, totally offended because he knew *my* middle name. I wasn't even sure how he found out. Probably at the barbeque at my parents' house. They were always using first and middle names. Sigh.

"Because it's lame."

"And *Athena* isn't lame?"

"I think Athena is a pretty great name, actually."

"My parents aren't here. You don't have to butt-kiss."

He laughed again. "I'm not trying to kiss anyone's ass. I really do like the name Athena."

"What's your middle name?" I tried again.

Tyler sighed. "Can't we just go to bed?"

"No," I insisted. "Tell me, tell me, tell me."

"Winston."

"Ha!" I barked out, then I contained myself. "Is it a family name?" I asked, knowing if it was, it could be a sensitive thing for him.

He groaned. "No, it's not a family name."

"Oh...well, it's nice. Very rich sounding. Winston," I tried it out. "Tyler Winston Scott. Not bad. You kind of sound important."

"Yeah, yeah. Now can we go to bed?"

"Is there something you're not telling me?"

"No."

"Tyler."

"There's not."

"Should I call Hannah?"

"You don't have her number."

"Actually, I do." I sat up and reached to retrieve my cell phone.

"I was named after the city where I was conceived."

"Winston?"

"Winston-Salem. My parents spared me the embarrassment by removing the Salem."

"What's Hannah's middle name?"

"Madison."

"Wisconsin?"

"Our parents traveled a lot."

"Random places…" I said, staring up at the dark ceiling.

"Yeah. Could've been worse, I suppose."

"How?"

"Could have been conceived here in New York."

"Ahh," I could see why that would be weird. "But maybe then you guys would have had other middle names. Like maybe they would have thought, 'We can't name the kids 'Tyler New York City' or 'Hannah Bronx,' and went with something like Anne and Robert."

"Tyler Robert Scott," he tried it out.

"I think I like Winston better."

"Me too," he agreed.

"What were your parents' names?"

"Tyler Manhattan and Hannah Bronx…we were named after them."

I laughed out loud and shoved his arm. "That's not even funny."

"Charles Randolph Scott and Annalise Edith Murray Scott."

"Annalise is pretty. Is Edith a family name?"

"Yeah…her grandmother."

"It is rather grandmotherly."

Tyler laughed. "Yeah, it is. What about your parents?"

"Katarina Melody Castellanos-"

"I knew a Castellanos. His name was Ed."

"I don't have a cousin Ed."

Tyler shrugged. "What about your dad?"

"Gregory Adrian Katsaros."

"That doesn't sound very Greek."

"Don't tell him that."

He chuckled. "We came from good stock, huh?

"I think so."

"Night, Spice."

"Good night, Ty."

- 24 -
Tyler

"You really like the desserts?" I asked Melanie. I was thinking about drafting a dessert only column as part of the series, but I wanted to make sure I had enough grilled dessert recipes to share.

"Yeah, they were great. You can probably even do a dessert pizza, right?"

"Ah, I love the way you think!" I leaned over and kissed her cheek. We were sitting on my bed. She was sketching some designs on her iPad and I was writing up some dessert recipes on my laptop. She looked so cute in her little dark-framed glasses.

I groaned. Planning this column was driving me crazy.

"What's the matter?" Mel asked, not moving her eyes away from her tablet.

"I just don't know if I should present it as a series or an ongoing column."

She set her tablet aside and gave me her full attention. "Well, if you present it to the magazine — any magazine — you're going to want it to be an ongoing opportunity, right? I mean you aren't going to want them to buy a series off of you for X amount of dollars and leave it at that? You're going to want some steady income."

"Yeah, I'd rather it not be a one and done thing."

"Then present it as an ongoing column. Each month you feature a new technique or course or recipe or whatever. Or you can feature different courses that all include the same technique? You can present the same recipe cooked across several grill types."

"That's a lot to think about."

"You'll figure it out. Just take your time and decide what works best for you and what makes the most sense for the long term. You'll want an idea that will stay fresh and stretch across time. Don't give away all your secrets at once."

"Thanks, babe."

"Of course," she smiled, then picked up her iPad and continued working.

Ever since she returned from Paris, we spent our nights together. Either she stayed at my place or I stayed at her place. Neither apartment was large enough for two people, and we really needed to have a conversation about that. I was ready to take that next step with Mel. I loved spending time with her and sharing our small spaces, but I wanted us to have something better. With what we were each spending on our tiny rooms, we could probably afford a studio or a one bedroom. *A bedroom with a door*, I mused, *what was that even like?*

"Do you want to move in together?"

Melanie froze.

I froze.

I hadn't meant to say that aloud. I mean, I meant what I asked, but I didn't mean to ask it. Not right at that moment at least. I didn't regret it though. It was what I wanted. I hoped it was what she wanted, too.

"Yes," she finally said. The word cutting through the silent space.

"What?" I asked, my eyes darting to her. "You do?"

"Yeah, I do."

"Really?"

She laughed. "Yes, really. Did you think I'd say no?"

I laughed, relieved that my little mistake hadn't blown up in my face. "I hoped you'd say yes. I was just thinking about it, and the question popped out. I hadn't meant to ask you right this moment, but I meant the question."

"I've been thinking about it, too."

"Really?"

"Yeah. I love being with you. And we're together all the time anyway."

"Right."

"It just makes sense."

"It does."

"This is so romantic."

"We'll have some cake and champagne later. I'll even buy you flowers," I told her as I moved our electronic devices off the bed.

"Oooh, daisies?"

"Whatever you'd like," I said, rolling on top of her. "We're moving in together."

"Yes," she said, smiling. "We sure are."

"This is going to be so much fun."

***

Melanie and I went to one of our favorite breakfast spots the following morning on our way to work. We'd begun taking overnight bags to each other's place instead of one of us rushing home to get ready in the morning before work. It sucked that we didn't have the space to store things at each other's apartments but planning ahead and taking an overnight bag worked just as well.

For now, at least. Soon we'd be moving in together.

In the light of day, I wasn't as nervous as I thought I'd be. I was excited about starting this new chapter with Mel. We'd need to work some things out, like when our lease terms ended and what we could afford with our salaries. But for now, we got to ride the high of deciding to take this monumental relationship step.

"Look," Melanie said, slapping an apartment magazine down on the table in front of me.

"They had those in the bathroom?" I asked, picking it up and flipping through.

"No," she said and pointed to the rack by the counter. "Over there. I know we haven't decided on anything, but I thought it might be fun to take a look at what's out there. See what our options might be."

I nodded. "Good idea." I looked at the index and flipped to the first page of the Manhattan listings. I knew that city real estate prices were going to be ridiculous in comparison to the other burroughs, but I couldn't imagine moving out of the city and I was pretty sure Melanie felt the same way. That was something we'd definitely need to talk about if the rent in Manhattan was too steep.

We spent breakfast flipping through the listings, pointing out the apartment features we liked and ones we didn't like. We talked about all the things we needed to talk about, like where we would choose to live if we couldn't afford to stay in the city. We shared our favorite neighborhoods, and the areas we wanted to steer clear of. It turned out that Melanie's lease was up in four months and mine was up in three, so we were both within the required time frame of letting our respective landlords know we'd be vacating.

In the end, we'd highlighted several properties we were interested in looking at in person and all but one of them were in the city.

Everything was going so well for us, and I couldn't help but look forward to what the future held.

- 25 -
Melanie

Tyler stabbed at the grilled chicken on his plate, not actually trying to lift it with his fork. I learned that about seven stabs ago; he would have accomplished that by now had it been his goal. Something was on his mind. Something he didn't want to talk to me about, but I had an idea of what it was. His boss, Roger, was publicly reprimanded by Preston for not producing anything innovative for the magazine. I was sure Roger was taking his frustrations out on Ty.

"Can I ask you a question?"

"You just did," he mumbled, seeming to come out of his haze a little bit. He looked at the shredded chicken with an odd expression, as though he didn't know how it got to be shredded when the rest was perfectly cubed.

"Ha-ha," I said, not amused with the semantics of the English language. "You've got some columns written now...why are you still staying at a job that you hate?"

He sighed. "It's not that simple, Mel."

Yeah. If his handy work with the chicken wasn't already an indication of his off mood, him calling me by a variation of my actual name was. He almost always called me Spice. I just wish he'd talk about it, instead of letting it fester.

"It can be that simple," I pushed. "Why not

present your idea to a cooking magazine, or even a lifestyle magazine? You could try for a column in one of the newspapers, too. There are possibilities out there, Tyler."

"You think I don't know that?"

"You don't act like it."

"You don't understand."

"I'm trying to understand, but you won't talk to me about it."

He sighed again. If he kept that up, he'd end up blowing everything off the table.

I looked at my watch. There wasn't enough time to have a deep discussion. We each had about fifteen minutes left of our lunch hour, and Tyler would be packing up and hauling ass in about five minutes. We might only be a couple minutes from our office building, but Tyler never returned to work late from lunch. He refused to give Roger fuel, whether he was in the office or not.

Case in point why Tyler needed to find a new job.

I piled my silverware on my plate and fished out a few bills to pay our tab. Tyler glared at me as he took out his own wallet, and I tucked my money away. No use in poking the bear today.

As we walked back to the office, weaving through the crowded sidewalk, I couldn't help but ask again. It concerned me that he was so unhappy at his job and that Roger treated him so terribly. Tyler's brother-in-law owned the magazine, for crying out loud. What was happening was unacceptable, and the only person who had the power to do anything about it was Tyler.

"I don't understand why you at least won't tell

Preston. Obviously, he's concerned with Roger's performance. Now would actually be the perfect time-"

"I'm not telling Preston anything," Tyler snapped. "You don't get it, Melanie." At least he was speaking softly when he called me by my first name again. "You grew up in the suburbs with a normal, really great family. You're lucky."

I laughed. "There's no such thing as a normal family."

He grinned a little, and I was pleased to see that little bit of Tyler spark. "I'm just saying that you had a normal family dynamic. I didn't have that. My sister and her husband were essentially my parents, and as much as they loved having me around—and still do—I always felt like an outsider. I wasn't their kid. I was way too old to be their kid, and they were way too young to be my parents. But they took me in, and I appreciate that. This job...it's not the ideal situation, but it's stable for now. I got it on my own merits, and I'm taking care of myself. If I were to quit my job, Hannah would worry."

"You don't have to quit without another prospect, Ty."

"I know...but I'm just not sure what exactly I want to do with these columns and until I do, I don't want to make any rash decisions. Plus, if I left the magazine, Preston would want to know why. Then he'd probably be pissed at me for not telling him about Roger sooner, and I'm not sure I want to deal with that either."

"That's understandable, but I hate seeing you so upset. I know Roger's probably giving you hell since he got reamed out."

"You know about that?"

"The entire building is talking about that."

Tyler grinned. "It was epic. Roger was acting so blasé, like he had a handle on everything, and Preston flipped. He called him out on acting smug and started asking Roger questions he didn't know the answers to. Things he should have known, like circulation numbers. It was fantastic. Almost worth the extra bullshit he's been giving me."

We paused in front of our building, as we always did. Despite working for different magazines on different floors, we kept our personal relationship outside of the building. He gave me a soft, lingering kiss, before pulling me into his chest and wrapping his arms around me.

"I love you, my Spicy girl."

I grinned; my face still pressed against his chest. "I love you, too."

"I know you only want me to be happy. I've got this, okay? I'm not letting it consume me. I promise."

"Just your lunch…" I said, pulling away and looking up at him. The guy liked to eat, and the fact that he didn't finish his plate said something about his mood.

"I had a big breakfast," he lied, and I let him. He wanted me to let it go, so I let it go.

"Okay. How about dinner at my place tonight? I've got a project I'm almost done with, so I want to camp out with my sewing machine for a bit."

"Sounds good to me." He kissed my forehead, the tip of my nose, and then my lips.

"I'll see you later," I told him and winked. He returned the wink, which told me we were going to have some frisky time later. At least, I hoped we would.

Sigh.

I couldn't get enough of Tyler Winston Scott.

- 26 -
Tyler

"Here you go," I said, as I set Melanie's plate in front of her on the bed. The lights were dimmed and there were candles lit on the windowsill. It wasn't exactly fine dining, but it was still a candlelit dinner...right?

Melanie grumbled a thanks, focused solely on the embellishment she was sewing onto a blouse.

Embellishment and blouse...two terms I never thought I'd be able to define.

I went over to the small counter where I'd plugged in the electric grill and plated my food, then returned to the bed and sat next to Mel, careful not to shake the bed where she was seated with her legs crossed, carefully sewing by hand.

Melanie sniffed. Then she sniffed some more, eyes still glued to the delicate stitches.

I don't know what people think designers do, but she truly was an artist. I haven't seen her work much, but what I've seen her do since I arrived an hour ago is mesmerizing. The intricate beadwork she had sewn into the fabric...she'd even shown me some lace she'd made by hand. She was amazing.

"What's that smell?"

"Dinner."

She lifted her eyes to my plate. Then her eyes darted to the plate I'd set before her. "You made that?"

"Yes."

"In my apartment?"

"Yes."

"You're unbelievable."

I would have been concerned by her statement if it wasn't for the fact that she gently set her work down beside her, picked up the plate, and dug into the grilled shrimp kabob with gusto. I was speechless. Melanie didn't pull the food off the skewer; she ate off the stick like it was corn on the cob.

"What are you doing?"

"Eating," she said, looking at me like I was the crazy one.

"That's not how you eat a kabob."

"Actually, this *is* how I eat a kabob."

"Well, it's the wrong way."

She sighed. "It all goes in the same place; what difference does it make how I eat it?"

"You're supposed to take the food off the skewer."

"Says who?"

"Everyone in America."

"Doubtful." She rolled her eyes. "Does it really matter?"

"Yes."

"Of course, it does," she muttered under her breath. Aloud she said, "I do it this way because I can have a little bite of all the flavors."

"You can do that when they're off the skewer, too." Duh. "You know, like when you eat foods that weren't cooked on a skewer. You cut them up and have little bites of all the flavors."

"Ha-ha. My name is Tyler, and I'm a grilling

genius, and I know how to eat, and no one else does." She said in a ridiculous mockery of my voice.

"Oh yeah?" I said, chuckling at her silliness.

"Yup," she smirked.

"God, you're cute when you think you're right."

"Thanks, but my name's not God."

"You're quite full of yourself this evening, aren't you?"

"I'm just happy I'm nearly done with this design." She flexed her fingers. "I feel like I've been working on it forever. It has more detail than other pieces and I didn't think about how much more work it was going to be."

"I have absolute faith in you," I told her as I carefully slid the shrimp, onion slices, and pineapple off the skewer and onto my plate. I picked up my fork and stabbed a piece of shrimp; ate it. Then I repeated the procedure with the onion and the pineapple, looking pointedly at Melanie.

"How can you be so sweet and so obnoxious in the same moment?"

"Years of practice being a little brother." I smiled a toothy grin.

"You're adorable. I bet that face got you out of a ton of trouble when you were little."

"It's been getting me in and out of trouble for years."

"That doesn't surprise me one bit," she said, chewing on her kabob in her weird way. "Want to watch a movie?"

"Yeah. How about *Jurassic Park*?"

"I was thinking *Ghostbusters*." Her and her

damn eighties movies.

"*The Matrix.*"

"*Bill and Ted's Excellent Adventure.*"

"*Forrest Gump.*"

"*The Breakfast Club.*"

"*Scream.*"

"*The Goonies.*" I actually liked *The Goonies*. But I couldn't let her win.

"*Empire Records.* I cooked."

"That's not fair."

"I always let you win." Not true. We usually went back and forth until one of us either fell asleep or distracted the other with sex.

In fact…I moved our plates off the bed.

"You don't always let me win," she argued. "*Ferris Bueller.* And I wasn't finished with that."

"*Edward Scissorhands,*" I whispered into her ear before I nipped at her earlobe.

"*Back to the Future,*" she responded, her voice breathy.

"*Braveheart,*" I said, rolling over top of her.

"*E.T.*" Her eyes locked onto mine. They were filled with heat.

"*American Pie.*" I slipped my t-shirt off, then hers.

"I'm having a difficult time concentrating," she said, her eyes fluttering shut as I sucked on her nipple through her black lace bra.

"I win," I said as I moved to her other breast.

She moaned. "I don't even remember what we were talking about."

"A movie," I reminded her.

"Right...*Top Gun.*"

If my girl was still spouting off movie titles, I wasn't doing my job properly. I increased the intensity of my suckling, while also adding a little bit of hand action on the other side. Her mewls told me she was enjoying herself. And when she was enjoying herself, I enjoyed myself.

"Tyler," she moaned.

"Yeah baby?"

"Quit teasing me."

I smiled against her breast and took a playful nip.

Melanie growled and pushed up, rolling us so that she was on top of me.

"Oh, how the tables have turned…" she said, looking into my eyes. She ground against me once, twice.

It was my turn to groan.

"*Sixteen Candles*," she offered, grinding against me again.

"*The Sandlot*." Could. Not. Let. Her. Win.

"*Terminator*," she said, licking and nipping at my nipple. My goddamned weakness.

"Deal," I said, flipping her back over and peeling her shorts off. I barely had my own off before I was driving deep into her.

- 27 -
Melanie

Coffee.

Need all the coffee.

Oh, the sweet deliciousness.

I sipped the hot brew — thick and black, just how I liked it — and looked out my small apartment window at the brick and glass of the building across the street. Thank goodness for my hearty little Keurig. When you lived in a tiny apartment, you made do with tiny appliances, and windows, for that matter. I glanced over at the little electric grill Tyler had brought over to cook our dinner. He was so creative. How many people in New York City, and other cities, didn't bother with grilling because they didn't have an outdoor space for an outdoor grill? I really believed there was a niche there he could — and should — tap into.

I heard a rustle from behind me and turned around to check out the culprit. And check him out I did. Tyler was a picture of sexiness in the morning. His slightly messy hair was a little extra messy, and he always had the cutest pout on his face when he was starting to rouse. The sheet was down around his waist, the hint of that sexy V peeking out from underneath.

How did I get so lucky?

I would never suggest I wasn't good enough for Tyler, because girl power and all that, but guys that look like him with those lean, cut muscles just weren't supposed to exist in the wild. Or if they did, they were supposed to be so rare you didn't just stumble upon them in real life…or elevators. Sort of like those little white baby deer. You just didn't see them grazing on the side of the road.

Tyler's leg suddenly shot across the bed, and I laughed, glad I wasn't lying beside him because I would have been on the floor. He'd told me the first time I slept over his place that he occasionally suffered from leg cramps in his sleep, horrified that he might kick me in the night. I wasn't worried about it, and he never got me.

Maybe I calmed him…he certainly calmed me. Being with him made me stop and appreciate life. When my mind was racing with all the things I wanted to do, restricted by what I actually could do, he somehow managed to calm me. I'd had a few boyfriends over the years, but nothing as serious as what I had with Tyler. It was new and fresh, but it was all-encompassing. In a short period of time, we threaded our lives together so intricately that I wasn't quite sure how I would function without him.

"You should take a picture, it'll last longer."

My gaze shot from his abs to his eyes as a shy smile spread across my face. Why I was shy with his man, I'd never know. We'd seen and touched nearly every part of each other's bodies, there was absolutely nothing left to be shy about.

"You look so damn hot standing there in only my t-shirt." I felt my entire body heat up. "How long have you been awake?" he asked, lifting his cell from the small bedside table and tapping the screen.

Did I tell him I never really slept? I was so close to finishing the piece I was working on last night—an embellished shift dress—I could hardly fall asleep. It was the most stylish thing I'd made to date, while still sticking to my boho roots. I was in love.

"Earth to Melanie. Everything okay?"

"Sorry," I grimaced, moving to stand at the foot of the bed. "I worked most of the night."

He nodded his understanding. "Finish it?" he asked, sitting up and scooting to the end of the bed where I was.

"Yup," I said.

He smiled up at me and said "I'm proud of you." Then he wrapped his hands around my bare legs and rested his head against my belly.

"Thank you," I said, leaning forward to kiss the top of his head. I took one hand off my warm mug and ran my fingers through his hair, attempting to straighten the disarray. It was no use. He'd either need a shower, a hat, or a lot of product to tame the jungle on his head. I kind of liked it as it was evidence of our fun night. "What are you up to?" I asked as he began lifting the shirt I was wearing and kissing the skin underneath.

"It's Saturday…I think it's a stay in bed all day kind of day."

I glanced at my finished dress and decided he was right. There was no other place I wanted to be today than in his arms in my bed.

***

Later that evening, after watching *three* eighties movies—I did win our last word contest last night—and one nineties movie—I do know how to compromise—I modeled my new dress.

Tyler fingered the lace overlay along the hemline. "This is really cool. I can't believe you stitched it by hand."

"Me either," I admitted through a laugh. Lacing was something I was always practicing and trying to hone, but I'd never taken on an entire lower hemline before.

"It makes the whole dress fancy."

He wasn't wrong. The dress was dark blue, almost black, and the thick lace was dark cream. Along the neckline I'd sewn in some wooden beads that matched the lace. I wasn't sure how it would turn out, but I loved it. I was thinking about wearing it to work on Monday. Brianna sometimes commented on my outfits, particularly the dresses…maybe this would be an opening for that.

"You should wear it to work. Let your boss see it."

"I was just thinking that."

He smiled. "Then do it. Brianna likes you. I'm sure she would be happy to help you get your foot in the door. Does she know you have a background in fashion?"

I shrugged, checking myself out again in the floor-length mirror that hung on the back of my bathroom door. "I had it in my resume that I was taking classes." My job with the magazine paid for my fashion degree. "I never updated it to include my degree. Wouldn't have made any difference for an executive assistant."

"Well, this *will* make a difference," he said, tapping the shoulder of the dress.

"You really think so?" I asked, wringing my

hands together. I felt like I was ready to tell Brianna that it was *me* who made the outfits I wore all the time, but it was still a terrifying thing to admit out loud. What if she had only been saying she liked them because she was being kind?

"I know so. Hannah said so, too, remember?"

I nodded. His sister really liked my stuff. Last time we had dinner with her, she told me she would be my first customer. She wanted to commission some stuff, but I wasn't quite ready for that. I told her as much, and I also promised to let her know the moment I was open for business.

Looking at myself in the mirror, I thought, maybe it would be sooner than I knew.

- 28 -
Melanie

I sat nervously in my seat waiting for Brianna to arrive. Of course, I finally garnered the courage to broach the topic of my designs with her, and she was late. Brianna was *never* late. Maybe it was a sign. Maybe today *wasn't* the day to do this.

After a few more minutes of nervously typing on my keyboard, the door to our suite opened, and Brianna walked in. She was smiling as she greeted me, the grin a great contrast to the typical firm expression on her face. Maybe today *was* the day to say something to her about my designs. If only she left me an opening…

"Good morning, Brianna," I said.

"Gorgeous dress, is it one of ours?" she asked, eyeing me as she passed. She was referring to the samples sent to the magazine by designers to get Brianna's attention or to be used for photo shoots. Whatever wasn't used or kept by models was sent to storage in the basement.

"It's one of mine, actually."

Cue the record scratch as Brianna stopped dead in her tracks. I sat in my seat, clenching every single muscle in my body as I waited for her reaction.

Her head turned towards me slowly, and she eyed my dress through the clear plate glass of my desk. "Stand up," she said. The quiet calm of her voice sort of freaked me out. Had she thought I'd stolen an idea or something?

I did as she said and stood from my chair, then walked around the desk to stand before her. If I was doing this, I might as well be doing it.

"That lace work is beautiful…and so unique."

I squealed on the inside. "I stitched it myself."

Her eyes shot to mine and her stony expression faltered a moment, but only for a moment. "You *stitched* the lace?"

I nodded like a damned bobblehead, both excited over her attention to the detail and nervous over her attention to me.

"This is amazing. You do really great work. You made the entire piece?" She asked, touching one of the beads along the neck.

"I did."

"You do this a lot?"

I nodded, then found my voice. "I make most of what I wear."

Her eyes met mine again. "I had no idea. Why didn't you tell me?" If I didn't know any better, I would have thought I had hurt her feelings. It wasn't that Brianna didn't have feelings--she was human after all--it was just that she wanted to know why I didn't tell her. I knew better than anyone that people in the industry were always throwing their products and samples at Brianna, so why wouldn't I have done the same since I had the most access to her? Well, for one thing I respected her too much. Also, I was terrified of being rejected.

"We need to talk about this," she said, giving me a small smile now. "Lunch, today."

"You have lunch with the representative from

Bloomingdale's about the advertising campaign."

"Reschedule it," she said before she disappeared behind her office door.

Reschedule it. It might not seem like that big a deal, but that advertising campaign is worth hundreds of thousands of dollars, if not more.

Holy shit.

***

"Ty!" I said, bursting into his apartment after work that day. Brianna and I had taken an extended lunch, so I ended up staying late to finish up the work I missed while we were out. I'd sent Tyler a quick text earlier letting him know I would meet him at his place when I got done.

"Hey, Spice," he said, looking up at me from the computer resting on his lap. He was leaning back against his headboard, dressed in nothing but a pair of pajama pants and a smile. Just how I liked him.

I bounced onto the bed, landing on my knees and straddling his legs. The bed banged against the floor and he laughed, setting his computer aside and gripping my legs behind the knee to pull me up to his lap. "Good news?" He knew I had lunch with Brianna, but that was all.

"Great news," I said, feeling like my smile was going to split my face in two.

"Tell me all about it," he said, kissing the tip of my nose.

I rested my arms over his shoulders, loving the intimacy of the position we were in. Face to face and chest to chest, but it wasn't sexual.

I told him how she complimented my dress

when she got to the office and how the invite to lunch happened. "I kind of thought she was upset with me for holding out on her all this time. She seemed a little disappointed I had kept it from her, but when I explained to her that I wanted to establish myself on my own merit and everything, she understood. She also said I was silly because getting started in the industry is all about who you know. Fortunately for me, I already know a lot of people."

"That's great, babe. It seems like she was very supportive."

"She was! And that's not even the best part." I didn't wait for him to respond. "She's going to set me up with a mentor. She knows so many people, and she has a few in mind that she trusts to steer me in the right direction—when I'm ready of course. I'm so not there yet, and I told her that. She said she thought it was smart that I knew my boundaries and all that. I just can't believe I was nervous about talking to her about it. She was amazing. And she loves my stuff. She told me she thinks I always wear the cutest things." I laughed. "I'm sorry. I'm just so wired."

"I can tell. I'm really proud of you, Spice."

I leaned my forehead against his. "Thanks. It means a lot to hear you say that."

"You hungry?" he asked.

"Yes," I practically growled. It was hours since lunch. "All I had at lunch was a salad with the tiniest piece of grilled salmon on it. It was good, but not filling at all. I was way too nervous to eat."

"My girl needs sustenance!" he said, making me laugh. "Let's order a pizza."

"That sounds perfect."

- 29 -
Tyler

"It's Tyler Scott, do you have a minute?"

I always used my first and last name when identifying myself to my asshole boss because most of the time he didn't remember which was which. If I used them both, there was a greater chance he'd recognize at least one of them.

"Come in," he called from behind the closed door. He sounded annoyed, but that wasn't new. He was always annoyed these days. I'd heard rumors his job was on the chopping block after Preston had given him hell. My brother-in-law was a laid-back guy, but he was serious about business. He wouldn't have made his fortune otherwise. He was also the kind of guy who strategized his next move; and I'm sure he had an entire chess game set up for Roger. I felt only a little guilty for not telling him just how much of an asshole Roger was, but I figured if the entire company knew, Preston had to know, too. If Roger had ever actually done anything damaging, I would have told Preston. No doubt about that. But so far, to my knowledge, all Roger was guilty of was cheating on his wife and not producing anything new for the magazine.

Which was precisely why I was knocking on his door.

Motivated by Melanie's success with her own

boss, I decided to present my column idea to Roger. Granted, Melanie and I had two very different bosses, but I thought Roger might have been feeling a little desperate given his reaming from Preston. He told him to come up with some new content…well, I was serving it to him on a grill. He could take it or leave it, but maybe he'd take it.

"What do you need?" he asked, his voice snide, as I walked in.

"I have a possible solution to the content problem," I said, portraying confidence I didn't actually feel. It wasn't that I was nervous, I just hated the bastard and hated that his useless piece of shit ass had decision-making power. I also knew that this entire situation, of me reporting to him, was of my own making. If I wanted Roger's job, Preston would have given it to me. That just wasn't how I wanted things to happen. I didn't want to be an editor. I wanted to grill and I wanted to write and this column…this column could help me to do just that.

"Oh yeah," he said, his gaze returning to the papers on his desk. His actions told me just how capable he thought I was of coming up with a solution to his problem. "And what's that?"

"*You're the Man* is full of pieces on sports, fitness, women, and fashion…but we don't have anything on food except the occasional summer barbecue article. I'm not suggesting we start adding recipes, but I think a regular food column that appeals to men would be a great addition to the magazine. For example," I continued when he hadn't yet interrupted me, "people don't think they can produce good quality grilled food from a city apartment, or any apartment really. I've come up with some ideas to prove them wrong."

Roger looked up then, made eye contact. Then he laughed. "That's your solution? You have some ideas about grilling in apartments? George Foreman came up with that solution years ago. Stop wasting my time."

I clenched my jaw and bit my tongue.

Asshole.

Without saying another word, I turned and walked out of his office. I stopped at my desk to shut down my monitor and grab my messenger bag.

Fuck this shit.

***

If you were wondering...I didn't quit my job. I should have, but I didn't. I went home that day and stayed there for an entire week. I had accrued enough sick and vacation time to support me for a little while. I left a message with Human Resources. Told them I had the flu. They'd call in a temp to support Roger while I was out. No big deal. He wouldn't even notice my absence.

My phone buzzed on my nightstand. I glanced at the screen. *Melanie.*

There was one other thing, too.

I hadn't talked to Melanie since that day.

At first, it was because I was too pissed off to function. I was afraid I'd do or say something I couldn't take back out of anger at Roger and she didn't deserve me projecting that onto her. So I responded to her phone call the day I walked out of Roger's office with a text that said I wasn't feeling well.

The next day I was still pissed at Roger.

The two days after that, I was pissed at her. Why did she get to have the awesome, supportive boss who was like a damn fairy godmother? She told her boss her dreams and BOOM! Wish granted. Like some crazy *I Dream of Jeanie* shit. I worked just as hard as she did, and I got the shit end of the stick.

I never said I was thinking rationally.

The shame came next.

First, I decided I was such a failure that I couldn't even successfully pitch an idea to a sinking ship of a magazine. Any size life raft would have done just fine, and I couldn't even make that happen. My proposal sank as though it were Preston's gigantic stainless-steel grill falling into his pool.

So, naturally, I determined that Melanie was way too good for me. She deserved so much better than an executive assistant. Never mind that she, too, was an executive assistant.

Again, I didn't have the most logical thought processes going on.

I was still spinning in the shame spiral, but now it was mostly because I was embarrassed for my behavior (or lack thereof) towards Melanie. I hadn't answered her calls or texts in days. She came to my apartment and knocked at least twice. I didn't answer. I'd given her a key a while back, but she didn't use it, and I was glad. I wasn't sure what I would have done if she walked in.

She deserved so much better than what I was— or wasn't—giving her.

- 30 -
Melanie

"These are fantastic," Heather, my potential mentor told me as she looked at a few of the shirts I'd brought with me. "What do you pair this one with?" she asked, holding up a sleeveless pink shirt.

"This denim skirt," I said, pulling said item out of my tote bag.

Heather looked impressed with my choice. "You've got a great eye and your designs are so fresh and fun." She set the skirt and top down on the table between us and looked at me. "Brianna speaks highly of you. She doesn't do that with a lot of people."

"I appreciate her support very much."

"She's an amazing woman. When she called and said she had someone she wanted me to mentor, I knew I had to meet you because Brianna wouldn't do that for just anyone. In fact, I wasn't sure she would do it for *anyone* until she did it for you."

"Well, I'm glad you decided to meet me. I honestly never expected things to get this far. When I talked to Brianna about everything, I never imagined she would open all these doors for me."

"Brianna Heatherly holds a lot of keys in the fashion industry. She's well-respected *and* people actually like her. She's a double threat," Heather smiled. "So tell me, Melanie, what are you thinking? What is it you want to do with your designs?"

I'd rehearsed my answer to this question seventeen times since I accepted the meeting with Heather Gregory. Heather was a freelance trend forecaster contracted by some of the most popular—and most expensive—fashion houses in New York City. I'd actually met her briefly in Paris, but I hadn't realized who she was until I stepped into her studio today. She was a short round woman with a sharp blonde bob and a kind face. I liked her immediately.

"I want my own fashion line," I said firmly. "I'd like to have a casual catalog as well as a professional catalog. This style already screams casual so that's a given, but I want to come up with items that can pass as business wear." I pulled the shift dress that started it all out of my tote. "Some more dresses like this and blouses that will go with simple pencil skirts."

"Professional boho-chic." Heather chewed on the words like she was trying them on for size. "I love it, and I love your work. I think you've got something here and I would love to work with you. Does Brianna have you meeting with anyone else?"

I couldn't contain my smile. After the week I'd had, I really needed this. "She hasn't set anything else up. She wanted me to talk to you first. She said we were kismet."

Heather laughed. "She would say that. What's your timeline?"

"I don't really have one. This has all happened so quickly. I'm committed to working for Brianna.

I don't have another source of income right now, so that's not something I can compromise on. I can put things together during my off hours, and hopefully grow to where this can be my primary focus."

Heather nodded. "I understand that, but I'd hate to see you spread yourself so thin between your line and the magazine. I'd really like for you to set some business goals for yourself and let's meet up again next week to discuss them. Then we can come up with a plan."

"That sounds wonderful, Heather. Thank you so much."

She stood from her seat and I followed suit. "You're so welcome. I love the energy that comes with a new project, and all this just screams energy. I'm honored to be part of this exciting time with you."

"Thank you for wanting to be part of it. You have no idea how much this means to me."

"Big things are going to happen for you, Melanie. I can see it now."

They had to, I thought to myself. Because I couldn't handle any more disappointment.

***

"Hey girl," my best friend said as I walked down the block away from Heather's office. "How was the meeting?"

"It was great," I told her, plugging my ear buds into my phone. It might have been 2019, but I loved my wired ear buds. Wireless could be so finicky, I preferred a good, wired connection.

"That's wonderful. I told you not to worry about it."

"I know, Mer. It's just been a rough week, so it was hard to relax."

"Still no word?"

"Radio silence."

I heard her sigh across the line. My sentiments exactly.

"I can't believe he ghosted you."

"Me either."

That was the understatement of the century. Things between Tyler and me had been awesome…until they suddenly weren't. We were talking about moving in together…looking at apartments even. The worst part of it was that I had no idea what went wrong. Had I done something? Was he bored? Sick? Dead? I didn't know.

Well, that wasn't entirely true. I knew he wasn't dead. In a moment of desperation, I reached out to Preston, and he said that as far as he knew, Tyler was fine. Which made me feel even shittier about the entire situation.

He was fine, and I was a damned mess.

"Earth to Melanie."

"Sorry! I was stuck in my head. What's up?"

"Are you coming home for your dad's birthday this weekend?"

"Yeah, I think so." Wasn't like I had other plans. Tyler was my social life in the city, and he was gone. Only he wasn't actually *gone*. He just wasn't talking to me for whatever reason.

I went from being upset to being pissed to being apathetic. If I was that inconsequential to him, then in return I shouldn't care, right? If he thought so little of me, shouldn't I think nothing of him?

I tried to think that way, I really did, but it was hard. I loved him. He told me he loved me, too. We had already slept together at that point, so it wasn't like he said it just to get in my pants. He had to have meant it, right?

He once told me he wasn't sure he knew how to love. It was the same night he told me he was afraid he was going to screw things up between us. The night he'd been afraid he already had screwed things up. I thought it was the saddest thing I'd ever heard.

But maybe he was right.

Maybe he didn't know how to love.

Because he was doing it all wrong.

- 31 -
Tyler

The banging on my door intensified as the minutes wore on. I cranked the volume on my nineties one-hit-wonder playlist to drown it out. Whoever it was would eventually go away.

"Little brother, if you don't open this door, I am going to call Preston and have him break. it. down." She enunciated the last three words.

Well, shit. It was only a matter of time before Hannah showed up. Had Melanie called her? No...she wouldn't have done that. Would she have?

I crawled out of the Tyler-sized dent in my bed and walked to the door. I heard my sister grunt as I began to slowly disengage the locks.

She banged again. "Pick up the pace." So impatient.

"Why are you being so harsh?" I asked as I opened the door. I didn't do anything to her.

"You called out of work all week, eh?" she asked, pushing past me into the room. She sure was in a mood, and I wasn't sure my apartment was big enough for both of us at that moment.

"How did you find out?" I asked, but I already knew the answer. I should have known Alice in Human Resources would tell on me. She was the only one in the entire organization who knew my relationship to Preston and that's because I had to list his wife—my sister—as my emergency contact.

"Melanie called Preston requesting proof of life on you. What the fuck is going on?"

My eyes widened for two reasons. First, Hannah *never* cursed. Ever. And second…Melanie called Preston for proof of life? "Proof of life? What are you talking about?"

"Why aren't you talking to Melanie?" I should have known she was here about my relationship and not my well-being.

I sighed, not wanting to get into it with my sister about Melanie. If I told her the entire story, I'd have to tell her about Roger. I didn't want to do that. "Things just aren't working out in that area of my life right now."

Understatement.

"Oh, Tyler. Stop being overdramatic."

"You think I'm being overdramatic? When an octopus gets upset, it eats itself. *That's* overdramatic."

"I don't think that's true," she said, tilting her head to the side in consideration of the random fact I'd spewed at her.

"Does it even matter, Hannah?" I asked, rubbing my eyes.

"You're throwing away a good thing, Tyler. Over nothing, most likely. I think it does matter."

"Yeah, yeah. One person in a relationship is always right. The other's male."

"You've always hid behind your humor, little brother. But I'm on to you," she said, pointing her finger at me.

She pushed past me again, this time towards the door.

"That's it…you're leaving?" I asked, surprised

she was letting me off this easy.

She looked around my apartment, and I knew what she was seeing: old take-out containers and an assortment of empty cans and bottles. "Tyler," my name came out on a resigned sigh. "I think you know you screwed things up with Melanie and you're punishing yourself enough. You don't need my help realizing that. Do I wish you'd talk to me? Of course. Am I going to make you? No. You're an adult. You need to start figuring this shit out for yourself. I love you, but I can't make you grow up."

With that, she left the apartment, the latch clicking quietly behind her.

Silence filled the room.

I looked around, and for the first time in days, I was disgusted with what I saw. I flashed back to a little more than a week ago when Melanie burst in excited to share the news about her meeting with Brianna. I remembered how happy we were and how we made love three times that night.

Love.

I *loved* that girl, and I let her go.

I screwed up again, and this time, I wasn't sure I'd be able to fix it.

- 32 -
Melanie

I wanted to hate the mixed tape Tyler had made me back when things were good. I listened to it here and there over the months we were together simply because it had been a gift from him. It had some of his favorite songs on it and I wanted to know everything about him.

These days I was listening to it just to feel close to him. I pressed stop on my very old Walkman and ejected the tape, not wanting to listen to one more one-hit-wonder. I twirled the cassette between my fingers for a minute before tossing it to the foot of the bed. The Walkman followed. Out of sight, out of mind, right?

Maybe I was pathetic…but I missed him. For him to go from being such a large part of my life to not existing in it at all was too difficult for me to comprehend. I wanted to hate him, but I couldn't. I was still so deeply in love with him, and maybe it was a lack of closure that kept me feeling that way. Maybe once I knew why he wasn't speaking to me, I'd be able to move on. Maybe I'd even hate him like I probably should.

The truth was…I didn't want to move on, and I didn't want to hate him. I wanted to go back. I wanted things to be exactly as they had been when my life was seemingly perfect. I had the guy and my dream job was falling into my lap…then it all went crashing down.

I checked the clock on my bedside table. It read four in the morning. I had been pulling all-nighters the last three weekends to get some more designs together to build my portfolio. Heather and I had reviewed my goals and were now working on putting together lists of vendors. I'd learned some of the business side of fashion through my job at the magazine and school, but it was a whole different reality when I was doing it for myself.

But this was what I had been working for. This was my dream.

I made wish lists of the various fabrics I wanted to get my hands on. The colors and patterns, too. I wanted mannequins and sewing machines and spools of thread in all the colors I could think of. Measuring tapes and needles and beads…I couldn't forget the beads. Also an assortment of strings would be great. I felt like that spoiled girl from *Charlie and the Chocolate Factory*. I wanted it all and I wanted it now.

Heather also recommended I find an investor so I could get started as soon as possible. I gave her a funny look as I wondered who on earth would invest in a no-name fashion designer, but she assured me that people did just that, and that I wasn't a no-name with both her support and the support of Brianna. I still didn't like the idea of riding on their coattails, but I was starting to not hate it at least. It was just the way things were.

As I finished yet another list, my mind drifted back to Tyler, as it always did.

I wondered if *I* tried hard enough.

He asked me not to let him screw up again.

Practically begged me. Did I let him screw up? Should I have used the key he gave me one of those times I went to his apartment? What if I had? What if I went inside and he still didn't want to see me? That would have hurt worse, I thought.

What if.

What if.

What if.

Ugh.

I couldn't concentrate.

Part of that was due to the hour, the other part was due to Tyler.

At least he was back at work after spending two weeks out with the "flu." In the weeks since he'd been back, I still hadn't seen him once. I looked for him in the elevator, but he must have been taking the stairs. I even rode the car all the way up one day, just to see if I'd spot him on his floor when the doors opened. I didn't see him, but I had seen Preston when I reached the top level and he gave me a questioning look. I just shrugged and mumbled something about missing my floor.

I moved my notebook to the nightstand and turned off the light, drowning the room in darkness.

It was strange, the darkness. Usually when I turned off the light inside my apartment, the lights from the city would cast a dim light across my space...but tonight there was nothing.

No light.

It was pitch black.

- 33 -
Tyler

3:25

3:29

3:34

3:35

3:36

Every single day in the office was a race against the clock. Could I make it to five o'clock without running into Melanie?

I messed everything up with her over nothing. She was the best thing I ever had. The worst part is that I hadn't even attempted to grovel yet, and she at least deserved that. Even if she didn't give me a chance. She deserved for me to get down on my knees and apologize and beg for forgiveness. I wouldn't blame her one bit for denying me. But she deserved that opportunity.

3:47

3:51

"Excuse me?"

I looked up from the time in the lower right corner of my computer screen to see an unfamiliar, clean-cut guy in a suit looking nervously at me from across my desk. "Can I help you?" I asked. I hadn't been expecting anyone and Roger never had appointments with men in his office.

"I have a four o'clock meeting with Roger Hoffstadt."

I pulled up Roger's calendar in my computer—the one he never used—and confirmed that there was nothing on his schedule. "I don't see anything on Mr. Hoffstadt's schedule. May I ask what this is in reference to?" I asked, picking up the telephone to page Roger's desk. I was still avoiding speaking to him in person when possible. Given that I rarely saw him before he pissed on my pitch, it wasn't that difficult.

The guy shifted nervously, and I was sure Roger's reputation had preceded him. "I'm a chef," he started...and my hand holding the phone froze. "I'm here to interview for the new *Grilling in the City* column."

My blood ran cold.

Then it ran hot.

So hot.

I slammed the phone down on the desk, not even taking care to place it back on the receiver.

I was done.

I stood so fast, my chair shot out from behind me and hit the wall with a deafening thud.

"After everything I've fucking done. This is how it goes."

"Excuse me?" Nervous Guy asked.

"I wasn't talking to you," I said, pointing at him. "If I were you, I'd run far the fuck away from here. Roger Hoffstadt will chew you up and spit you out."

I turned away from him and stomped over to Roger's door, swinging it open. The opaque glass shattered when the door hit the wall.

"What do you think you're doing?" Roger yelled, standing from behind his desk.

"Fuck you," I said snidely. "You are the biggest

piece of shit. *Grilling in the City*? Who is the writer? George Foreman?"

Roger sneered. "Who do you think you are? You think you could write it? You're an assistant. You're my assistant. And you're fucking fired."

"Wrong," I said, pulling my cell phone from my pocket. I tapped the screen and held the phone to my ear.

Roger picked up his desk phone. "Yeah I need security to YTM, suite two-one-one."

When my call connected, my eyes seared Roger's. "Preston, we need to talk."

***

"I can't believe he was such a shit to you, and you didn't say anything," Hannah said, retrieving three Modelos from the refrigerator and popping the tops. She gave one to me and one to Preston before nestling in beside him on the couch with her own bottle of beer. It was Taco Tuesday, and Hannah was nothing if not consistent in her themes. Taco night meant Mexican beer.

"You know how I feel about nepotism," I said, taking a long pull from my bottle.

"Nepotism has nothing to do with it. It's about human decency. Anyone else would have filed a complaint with Human Resources. You should have said something. It infuriates me that he got away with so much."

"He didn't get away with that much, babe," Preston said.

"He treated Tyler like shit."

"He treated everyone like shit," I said. "I was just the person who was in contact with him the most."

"Doesn't make it right. And he was taking your idea…" she trailed off, making a face.

"He was on his last leg and he knew it," Preston said. "He was set to present a new idea to me tomorrow morning. Had he come to me with that grilling column, I would have known exactly where it came from and had he not given credit where credit was due, I would have fired him on the spot."

"Well at least it didn't have to come to that," Hannah said.

"I would have rather it came to that then the shit show this afternoon," Preston said, referring to what had happened once Roger realized who I had called.

"Preston? Preston Parks? What are you, a fucking narc?"

Roger didn't realize I hadn't hung up on Preston, I just changed my cell phone to speaker. He could hear everything he said.

"Have you been telling him everything? Did you run crying to him when I turned down your column idea? You don't know shit. You're a kid. What the hell do you know? You think you can write that column? You think you can grill?"

"I think I already did *write that column, and I* know *I can grill. I have a journalism degree, dickhead. I'm not* just *an executive assistant. And fuck you for undervaluing that position. Administrative support staff are some of the most valuable members of an organization. They're also some of the most powerful ones."*

"Yeah…because they have the boss on speed dial."

"Roger," Preston said, walking in the office and taking in the mess of glass by the door.

I winced, really noticing the pile of glass for the first time. I should have been more careful, but I hadn't been thinking at the time.

"Should I come back later?" We all turned toward the doorway where Nervous Guy was standing.

"Who the fuck are you?" Roger asked.

Preston glared at him. "Mr. Hoffstadt, I don't think I should have to tell you not to speak to guests in my building that way."

"I'm here for an interview."

Preston approached him. "I apologize for the inconvenience, but any business you have here with Mr. Hoffstadt today will need to be placed on hold. Please take the elevator up to the eighteenth floor and give the receptionist, Karen, your contact information. I'll follow up with you." Nervous Guy was smart enough to high-tail it out of there after that, and Preston's attention returned to Roger.

"Mr. Hoffstadt, I'm afraid your employment at Parks Publishing has come to a close. I'd appreciate it if you'd quietly pack your personal effects and leave immediately. Your final paycheck will be sent to you."

"Are you fucking kidding me?" Roger spit the words out. "All because of some kid?"

Preston walked right up to Roger, causing him to take a step back. "I hold my management team to a very high standard. A standard you have been beneath for entirely too long. I tolerated your nonsense because you were producing, but now you're not. I also do not tolerate any of my employees speaking to any of my other employees the way I have just witnessed. You're dragging the magazine down with your rotten attitude, and I'm finished with it."

"I've given this magazine five years."

"And you'll give it no more." Preston looked at me. "Tyler, go get Mr. Hoffstadt a box for his personal belongings."

I nodded, passing two security officers on my way out of Roger's office. I laughed to myself, thinking about how Roger called his own personal escort out of the building.

"And you did it all without letting the cat out of the bag about Tyler being family," Hannah said.

"It was important to him," Preston said, and I respected him even more for it.

"You're sweet," she said, kissing his cheek.

Seeing them cuddling and kissing made me yearn for Melanie. The last time I was over their house for Taco Tuesday, Melanie was with me. I missed her so much.

It was time.

"Han," she stopped making goo-goo eyes at Preston and looked at me. "I need your help."

- 34 -
Melanie

I sat at my desk, keying in some final notes for Brianna's upcoming travel itinerary when the suite door opened. Glancing at the clock on my computer monitor, I saw that it was ten minutes until six. I wasn't expecting anyone.

Hannah peeked her head around the corner and smiled when she saw me.

My heart raced.

What was she doing here?

"Hey, girl," she said, walking up to my desk like her brother hadn't broken my heart.

"H-hi," I stuttered, unsure of what she could possibly want.

"I just wanted to drop this off for you," she said, dropping a folded square of paper on the desk in front of me. "I'll see you later," she sang, disappearing back out the door as quickly as she'd walked in.

Did that even happen? Had she been a figment of my imagination?

I looked down at my desk, eyeing the paper. It looked like a folded-up note, like the ones you passed to your friends in high school before texting.

I took it between two fingers, holding it up to eye level. There was writing on the inside. My heart told me it was Tyler. Duh. Who else would have sent me a note through Hannah?

I quickly unwrapped the note and a slip of paper fell to the desk. I ignored it and read.

> *Spice,*
> *I can't properly express how sorry I am for my behavior, or lack thereof, the last few weeks. I'm not going to offer you excuses, you deserved so much more from me than that, though someday I would like to explain what happened. I'm not so good with these kinds of words, but I'm trying here…*
>
> *If radio stations still took dedications, I'd dedicate all the love songs to you…like Savage Garden's "Truly Madly Deeply" or "I'll Be" by Edwin McCain. I want to take you on dates to the mall and have matching instant messenger usernames. I'd also keep making you mixed tapes of all the songs that make me think of you. Then I'll make more that make me think of us.*
>
> *I'm sorry, Melanie. I miss you so much. Please come see me tonight at 10:00pm.*
> *Love,*
> *Tyler*

I picked up the fallen piece of paper. It was a ticket to the Empire State Building's 86th floor observation deck. He was inviting me to the top of the Empire State Building.

***

"How very nineties of him," Meredith said when I called her to tell her about Tyler's note on my way home.

It was very *Sleepless in Seattle* of him, I silently agreed, leaning back in my seat. I'd ordered a company car--something I never, ever did--but I just wanted to sit and chill and process and talk to my friend and I couldn't do that while battling the Subway. I figured I was owed the favor since the owner of the company's wife had just dropped a bomb on my desk.

"Should I go?"

"Do you want to go?" she countered.

I sighed. I wanted her to just tell me what to do. I didn't want to have to think about it. That's why I called my best friend. I wanted her to give me the answer.

"I do and I don't."

"Explain."

"I want closure, but I don't know if I want to see him."

"That's understandable."

"I just feel like I should go, you know? You should always respond to the grand gesture."

"Since you can't see me, I'm gonna tell you...I'm rolling my eyes."

"I would just hate for him to be waiting up there for me, and I don't show up."

"Well, he should have thought about that before he ditched you." I winced at her harshness. "Listen sweetie, your heart is way too big. I know you're really undecided about what to do here, or pretending to be undecided, because you still love him. You've always been a hopeless romantic. You know...you can go there tonight--respond to the grand gesture--and not actually take him back. You can thank him for the effort, forgive him even, but still say no. You don't have to respond to the grand gesture the way they do in all those movies you watch."

Maybe she was right. Maybe I could just go there and talk to him and we could leave as friends. Or not friends. Maybe we could just make peace.

"Or you could just not go and let him know what it feels like to be ghosted." Ah, there she was. "That's my vote, for what it's worth."

"I was beginning to think you'd gone soft," I told her.

"Me? Nah."

I laughed, appreciating the comfort of my friend, but still not feeling any closer to a decision.

- 35 -
Tyler

I'd never been so nervous in my entire life.

It wasn't only because I was eighty-six stories up in the sky and terrified of heights. That was certainly an important factor, but it wasn't the only factor. I was laying it all out on the line tonight. I was laying myself bare, and I was doing it publicly. That was a very special kind of terrifying.

I let the security guards know what I was up to so they wouldn't try to chase me away or call me in for loitering or anything else. One looked at me like I was crazy anyway, the other looked at me with pity in his eyes. Clearly neither one of them were romantics.

As it neared ten o'clock, I alternated between standing off to the side of the elevator and walking around the deck. I wasn't sure if I should be waiting right there for her to see me right away, or if another position would be better. Then I worried about the view...was one side of the Empire State Building better than the other? And where were they in the movie?

Did it matter? Not really.

And none of it would matter if she didn't show up.

Shit.

I hadn't actually considered the fact that she

might not show up. When Hannah helped me cook up this plan, it didn't even dawn on me that she might not come. I was certain she'd show up. *Everyone* showed up for the grand gestures. That's the way the movies worked. They were romance movies for a reason. If the grand gesture failed, it was a tragedy, not a romance.

But we didn't live in a damned romance movie.

Why hadn't I considered that?

I ran my hands down my face and groaned, bumping the person standing next to me. "Sorry," I mumbled.

"It's okay," she said.

I turned to head back towards the elevator but paused.

That voice.

I knew that voice.

I turned around and looked at the woman I'd bumped into.

It was her.

Melanie.

"You came." I looked into her eyes, shaking my head.

She shrugged. "I'm not entirely sure why I'm here."

My heart dropped to my gut.

Then I remembered my next move.

"Wait," I told her, holding up my hand.

She gave me an odd look--as did a few other people--as I dug around my pocket for my cell phone. Where the hell was it?

"Ah-ha," I said, pulling it out of my jacket pocket. I tapped the screen a few times, pulling up the music app and pressing play.

Then I held my cell phone above my head.

Melanie

My eyes widened as the first few notes of Peter Gabriel's "In Your Eyes" played through Tyler's cell phone.

My cheeks heated from the attention we were drawing--as did his--but he didn't falter.

I smiled shyly, shaking my head at the scene before me. He was so ridiculous. Leave it to Tyler to top one romantic gesture with another.

He lowered his cell phone and cut off the music, taking a tentative step towards me. "I'm sorry for everything."

"I know," I said, nodding my head. "I know you are."

I could see it in his eyes. That scared little boy was in there somewhere, but he looked a little bit stronger than the last time I'd seen him.

He pulled me into his chest, and I pressed my cheek against his heart, winding my arms around his body.

"You make me want to be a better man," he said, and I laughed.

"That's enough of the pop culture references, Ty," I said, pulling back and looking up at him. "Let's just be me and you, okay?"

"There's no two people I'd rather be."

I smiled and he held me close again, resting his chin on the top of my head.

"Things went sideways at work," he started telling me, and I shook my head to stop him. There would be time for explanations later, but I didn't want to hear them now. Not in this moment.

"Whatever spooked you, it doesn't matter. What matters is how you handled it."

"I handled it really poorly."

"You're supposed to lean on me when things get rough, no matter what they are."

"I know," he said, his voice pained. "I'm sorry I turned away from you when I should have turned towards you."

"If this is going to work, we need to communicate."

"Baby, I'm going to communicate with you so much you're going to get sick of me."

I rolled my eyes at him. "You're a dork, Tyler Winston Scott. But you're my dork, and I'll never get sick of you."

"What did I do to deserve you?" he asked, looking at me like I'd hung the moon and all the stars.

"Nothing special, Ty. Just keep being you. That's who I fell in love with. That's who I want to be with. You don't have to do anything fancy. Just be honest with me. And don't get spooked," I added that last part while stabbing him in the stomach with my finger.

"I won't. Never again. I promise."

"I love you," I told him, losing myself in his baby blue eyes.

"I love you more," he said, and then he pressed his lips against mine.

Epilogue
Melanie

Flashing lights.
People everywhere.
Applause, oohs, and aahs.
All the colors of the rainbow.
And it was all for me.
Athena by Melanie Katsaros was a hit. I had my own personal show at New York's fashion week--albeit a small show--and I was standing at the end of the runway, flanked by models, being given a standing ovation. Front and center in the crowd were my people...Brianna, Heather, Hannah, Preston, Meredith, and Tyler. The only thing missing was my parents, but this so wasn't their thing. I'd invited them, but knew they'd decline the invite.

Tears streamed down my face as I took it all in...as I absorbed what that moment meant. I had made it.

A sneak peek at my collection by some buyers from three of the major department stores and even more smaller boutiques already had offers flowing in. At this rate, I'd be able to pay off my investor in one lump sum, though he'd never accept it all at once. Preston was way too kind to accept anything more than our pre-arranged, no-interest, payment plan. And before *I* get accused of nepotism, Brianna arranged the investment without my knowledge. She hadn't told Preston who he was investing in, just that she "had a designer." She didn't even know about me and Tyler, or about Tyler and Preston. Everything just sort of worked out.

My life was absolutely perfect.

Tyler was also perfect, and up on his luck. He finally accepted Preston's help...well, as much as he would accept it. He pitched his column idea to the new editor-in-chief of *You're the Man* and he loved it. "Urban Grilling" had been being published for almost a year now, and it got rave reviews from even the toughest critics. Celebrity chefs even tried Tyler's techniques and requested to do guest pieces.

Everything was finally coming together.

Stepping behind the curtain of the runway, I stopped to take it all in once again. The dressing room was in complete disarray. Scraps of clothing were everywhere, and people were still bustling around, only slower now, without the preshow frenzy.

It was over, and I felt energized and relieved and elated and calm all at once. It was a heady feeling.

"It was amazing!" Meredith squealed as she appeared behind the curtain. My people had all-access VIP passes so they could calm me down before the show--and after-- if I needed it.

I squealed my happiness in return and the two of us bounced up and down, garnering attention from others in the room. People in fashion were so blasé, but I was not. I was so excited, and I just couldn't hide it.

"You did great, Spice. It was amazing." Tyler came over and kissed my forehead. "I'm so proud of you. I can't wait to get you home," he'd whispered that last part. And yes, we'd finally moved in together. It was a smallish one-bedroom apartment, but it was on the upper east side of Manhattan and it had a balcony — bonus! So naturally we had a grill.

"We are proud of you, too," Brianna said, speaking for her and Heather. "It was an absolute success."

"Amazing first show," Heather added. "I've already gotten several email inquiries."

"I still want to be your first customer," Hannah said, as she and Preston filed in last.

Well…I thought they were last, but…

"Mom?"

Fresh tears streamed down my cheeks as my mom and dad appeared from behind the curtain. "We're so proud of you, Melanie," she said.

"I can't believe you put all of this together," my dad said, looking around at all the shirts, skirts, and dresses tossed around the room. He'd always been the toughest critic of my dreams, but I knew it was only because he didn't understand what it was that I was doing. Now he did.

I ran over and hugged both my parents, then I made my way down the line, hugging everyone else. My people.

As I turned back towards Tyler, I gasped.

He was down on his knee.

In front of our closest friends and family.

Our people.

"Melanie Katsaros," he began. "When I met you, I didn't really understand what love was, but you helped me learn. Every day since then, you taught me to fall in love with you more and more and I'm not sure I even remember what my life was like without you in it. That's probably because it wasn't much of a life at all. Almost all my dreams—our dreams—have come true. All but one. So what do you say, Melanie? Put me out of my misery once and for all? I mean, come on...we put together IKEA furniture and only threatened to kill each other once. If that's not love, I don't know what is." A tear slipped down my cheek and I hastily wiped it away. "I want to spend the rest of my life trying to get out of debt with you, Mel. Seriously though, because I bet you're about to make bank with all this." He waved his hands around at the colorful designs hanging discarded on wire racks all around us. All my hard work--still surreal. "You're amazing, baby. Simply irresistible.

What do you say?"
   "I say yes."

THE END.

.

Tyler's 90s Mixed Tape

Now That We Found Love - Heavy D & The Boyz
Lovefool - The Cardigans
Wannabe - Spice Girls
No Scrubs - TLC
Here Comes the Hotstepper – Ini Kamoze
Enter Sandman – Metallica
I'm Gonna Be (500 Miles) – The Proclaimers
Baby Got Back – Sir Mix-a-Lot
Bitter Sweet Symphony – The Verve
I Want It That Way - Backstreet Boys
Smells Like Teen Spirit – Nirvana
Bye Bye Bye - *NSync
Ice, Ice, Baby – Vanilla Ice
What's Up – Four Non Blondes
U Can't Touch This – MC Hammer
Gangster's Paradise – Coolio

Melanie's 80s Mixed Tape

Don't Stop Believing – Journey
Just a Friend – Biz Markie
Walk Like an Egyptian – The Bangles
Girls Just Want to Have Fun – Cyndi Lauper
Free Fallin' – Tom Petty
Our Lips are Sealed – The Go-Gos
It Must Have Been Love – Roxette
Livin' on a Prayer – Bon Jovi
Fight For Your Right – Beastie Boys
Alone – Heart
Your Love – The Outfield
Manic Monday – The Bangles
It's Tricky – Run DMC
Eye of the Tiger – Survivor
We Built This City - Starship
Sweet Child O' Mine - Guns N' Roses

Acknowledgements

First and foremost, I want to thank Cassy Roop of Pink Ink Designs for designing the cover that was the basis for this story. It was love at first sight for me, and several ideas later, Simply Irresistible was born. Thank you to my editor and friend, Aimee Lukas. Thank you, Natasha Carrere, for the proofreading. You two ladies make the editing and final review process easy. Thank you to my Chapter Chicks...you guys give me motivation, names, ideas, and so much more. Last, but certainly not least...thank you to my family for your ongoing support! My husband, parents, siblings, niece, and so on.

About the Author

Jennifer was born and raised on Long Island, in New York. She relocated to South Carolina in 2002, where she met the love of her life. They got married in 2008, and live their happily ever after just outside of Charleston with their fur-kid. When she's not reading or writing, she works as a behavioral therapist, and is also a graduate student, pursuing a Master Degree in Psychology as well as a Graduate Certificate in Behavior Intervention in Autism. She enjoys amateur photography, traveling, and music…it's a bonus when she can combine all three. Jennifer is also a breast cancer survivor, having been diagnosed in 2017 and declared cancer-free in 2018. She independently published her debut novel, *Our Moon (JACT 1)*, in June 2015.

Connect With Me

Email: jenniferlallenauthor@gmail.com
Website: www.jenniferlallenauthor.com
Facebook: www.facebook.com/Jallenauthor
Twitter: https://twitter.com/AuthorJenniferA
Mailing List: http://eepurl.com/b4LjgD

Also by Jennifer L. Allen

www.ingramcontent.com/pod-product-compliance
Lightning Source LLC
Chambersburg PA
CBHW020632180626
46816CB00003B/923